Hamburgers, Homicide and a Honeymoon

The Charlotte Denver Cozy Mystery Series
Book 5

Sherri Bryan

Sherri Bryan

CONTENTS

Cast of Characters 4
Prologue 6
Chapter 1 9
Chapter 2 31
Chapter 3 46
Chapter 4 65
Chapter 5 77
Chapter 6 93
Chapter 7 105
Chapter 8 120
Chapter 9 144
Chapter 10 164
Chapter 11 174
Chapter 12 185
Epilogue 200
Other Books by Sherri Bryan 227
A Selection of Recipes from this Book 228
Note from Sherri 235
About Sherri Bryan 236
Acknowledgements 237
All Rights Reserved 238

CAST OF CHARACTERS

Charlotte Costello (née Denver) - Owner of *Charlotte's Plaice* café on the marina in St. Eves.

Nathan Costello - Detective Chief Inspector at the St. Eves police department. Also Charlotte's husband.

Jess Beddington – Charlotte's closest friend and co-worker at *Charlotte's Plaice*.

Detective Sergeant Ben Dillon - Also Jess's boyfriend.

Detective Sergeant Fiona Farrell – DS in the St. Eves police force.

Amanda – Nathan's assistant

Ava Whittington - Lifelong resident of St. Eves. Has known Charlotte since she was born.

Harriett Lawley - as above.

Betty Tubbs - as above.

Leo Reeves - lifelong resident of St. Eves.

Harry Jenkins - lifelong resident of St. Eves.

Garrett Walton - Lifelong resident of St. Eves and skipper of one of St. Eves fishing boat fleet. Also Charlotte's godfather.

Laura Walton - Garrett's wife and Charlotte's godmother.

Yolanda - Owner of the Mini-Mart on the marina.

Aidan Pitt – Ex-TV financial advice expert and entrepreneur

Ruby Pitt – Aidan's wife

Frankie Ingram – Local tattooist

Amy Baker – St. Eves resident

Penny Baker – St. Eves resident and Owen's girlfriend

Hamburgers, Homicide and a Honeymoon

Owen Fisher – St. Eves resident Penny's boyfriend
Zac – Penny and Owen's son
Eddie Lewis – Aidan Pitt's assistant
Georgina Lewis – Eddie's mum
Danny Fisher – Owen's cousin
Susan Fisher – Danny's wife
Big Al – Burger bar owner
Detective Inspector Toby Carter – London police detective
Detective Sergeant Ken Rafferty – London police detective
Cindy Powell – Co founder of 'The Pittettes'
Brenda Tatum – Co founder of 'The Pittettes'
Josie – Tattooist at Ingram's Ink
Giles – Tattooist at Ingram's Ink
Pippin - Charlotte's West Highland Terrier.

PROLOGUE

The man leaned his forehead against the cool glass of the window pane.

Eyes closed, he stood for a while, contemplating his situation, before looking in the mirror which hung between the window frames of his home study.

He ran his hand over his chin, suddenly weary. His reflection told him that, at 61, he still looked good. A few strands of grey peppered his otherwise-dark hair and his taut physique was confirmation that his strict exercise routine was paying off.

He had more money than he knew what to do with, a wife who turned the heads of men half his age, and the stamina of a thirty-year-old. He could party all night long when the occasion called for it, be up at five-thirty to go running, behind his desk by eight, and still run proverbial circles around anyone who dared to think they could get one over on him. Even on three hours' sleep, he was as sharp as a tack.

So why had she left him?

Moving to sit at his desk, he rested his chin on interlocked fingers. He opened a file on his laptop and clicked on a video within it. It began to play and he sat back in his chair, watching the woman he loved exit a cab outside the exclusive block which housed the luxury apartment he'd bought her.

She held an umbrella close to protect herself from the horizontal rain, but he didn't need to see her face to know it was her. As she leaned forward to get out of the car, he paused the video to zoom in on something he'd missed the first time he'd watched it. It was a tattoo he'd never seen before, revealed above the low neckline of her t-shirt.

Closer inspection confirmed it was a cherub, holding aloft a heart which enclosed the monogram AB & FI.

His jaw tensed and his knuckles whitened as his nails dug deep into his palms.

FI.

So she *was* seeing that lowlife. They'd always been close but she'd assured him there was nothing between them—that they were just friends. He should never have trusted her.

As images of them together flooded his thoughts, it took all his mental strength to push them away, the effort making him shudder.

His preoccupation with the situation was diverted when he clicked into his email. He stared at the message he'd received two weeks previously, his frustration growing.

I know what you did.

I know what you did all those years ago.

You have until the end of June to make amends with those you hurt so deeply.

If you fail to do so, I will go to the press with my story and you can kiss your reputation goodbye.

Remember—the end of June. Not a day later.

He was not easily intimidated but if there was one thing that scared him to his core, it was not being in control. The fact that two situations in as many weeks had left him feeling powerless didn't sit comfortably with him at all. Not at all.

Fixated on the message he banged his fist on the desk, causing the contents of his desk organiser to jump out of their neat compartments and onto the floor.

He pressed a button on his phone. "Look, what's the news on the email? Have you established its source? Damn it, I *have* to know who sent it. Keep on it, okay? I don't care how much overtime I have to pay you. Oh, and your weekend to London? You'll be pleased to know I'm coming with you, so get me on a flight. What? No, definitely not pleasure—strictly business. There's a little job I want you to do for me…"

He gave his instructions before settling back into his reclining leather chair. A gleaming bronze trophy sat on the corner of his desk and he ran his hand over it, a faint smile on his lips. The plaque on the statuette of a figure, arms raised in triumph, read 'Triathlon Champion 2002.' He prided himself on his ability to have beaten men half his age to win that trophy and, dented ego bolstered a little, he rewound the video.

The image of the love of his life with another man's initials tattooed on her body was intolerable.

So he would take steps to ensure he didn't have to tolerate it.

If he couldn't be with her, he would damned well see to it that no one else could either.

CHAPTER 1

"Are you sure we've got everything? Passports, tickets, money? Ohmigosh! Did I remember to unplug the iron?"

Charlotte Costello clambered into the back of the car, a frown creasing her brow.

"Look, will you please stop worrying?" said her husband, Nathan. "Everything's fine. We haven't forgotten anything, you didn't leave the iron on, Pippin's going to be fine with Leo, and *you* should be enjoying yourself. This honeymoon's supposed to be all about relaxing, not stressing out. And you've got the baby to think of now, remember."

"Er, you don't have to remind *me* about the baby, thank you." She fixed Nathan with a glare as she settled into the back seat for the drive to the airport. "I'm the one getting kicked like a football every five minutes."

Charlotte's friend, Jess Beddington, grinned at her in the interior mirror. "Well, you don't have to worry about the café while you're away because Laura and I will look after everything—we'll treat *Charlotte's Plaice* as if it was our own. And you'd better not be calling us every five minutes, either, to check everything's okay because, if you do, you're going to get on my nerves. Just enjoy your honeymoon and forget about St. Eves for two weeks."

Almost six months had passed since Charlotte Denver had become Charlotte Costello. A visit to Nathan's family in Wisconsin in the Midwest USA had always been their first choice for the honeymoon but, when Charlotte had announced her surprise pregnancy, they'd put the trip on hold until after the birth of the baby.

Instead, they'd opted to take their honeymoon in London—the capital city that Charlotte had only visited briefly, but which she longed to explore with Nathan while they still had some time to themselves. And, to start the trip in comfort, they were making the journey by air, flying from the local airport to London Gatwick.

"Oh, look! Charlotte, look!"

As Jess drove past the back of Charlotte's marina-front café, a send-off committee comprising her godparents—Garrett and Laura—and her dear friends, Ava, Harriett, Betty, Harry, and Leo, waved them off from the side of the road. As they all blew kisses and called out their best wishes for a happy honeymoon, Leo held Charlotte's West Highland Terrier, Pippin, in his arms and waved his paw up and down.

"Oh, that's so sweet of them! Oh, look at Pippin! Oh dear…" Charlotte delved into her bag for one of the many packs of tissues she'd become accustomed to carrying around.

Over the past few months her hormones had caught her out on numerous occasions, causing her to burst into floods of impromptu tears several times a day. She hoped that when they arrived in London and the honeymoon really began, the tears would abate.

"Jess, can you pull over for a minute, please?" Nathan said, unfastening his seatbelt.

"Oh! What is it? What did we forget?" Charlotte went into a mild panic.

"Nothing. We didn't forget anything. Everything's fine. I'm coming to sit in the back with you, that's all." He shuffled along the back seat and put his arm around her. "Come here." Taking a freshly-laundered handkerchief

Hamburgers, Homicide and a Honeymoon

from his pocket, he dried her tears. "Now, please. Will you try to relax and look forward to the next two weeks? We're going to have a fantastic holiday, you, me, and little baby Costello."

As she leaned against his chest, Charlotte felt all her anxiety melt away.

She closed her eyes and thought how lovely it was that her friends had made time to come and wave them off.

I'm so lucky, she thought as she drifted off into a light sleep. *And this holiday is going to be fabulous. Two weeks of relaxation and time to ourselves. We could both do with a rest.*

oooooo

The airport was buzzing. A busy Saturday afternoon guaranteed that every luggage trolley was conspicuous by its absence, and crowds of people mooching over departure boards and queuing to check-in, filled the terminal with the anticipation of exciting times ahead.

"Wait here a minute, I'm going to see if I can find a trolley." Nathan disappeared, leaving Charlotte with the bags.

It was a long time since she'd been in an airport. The last time had been when she'd arrived back from Spain with Garrett and Laura, following the death of her parents. She quickly put the memory from her mind.

As she sat on her case, watching the bustling hordes of travellers, it didn't escape her attention that a great number of them bore intricate tattoos.

A young woman with a smooth, ash-blonde, asymmetric haircut caught her eye. Sitting on a bench beside the group with whom she appeared to be travelling, she was making cooing noises at an endearingly podgy toddler with a shock of ginger hair. As the baby clung to her sleeve, she shrugged out of her jacket to reveal a series of striking tattoos running from her hand to her shoulder, depicting the various stages of a butterfly as it emerged from its dull chrysalis into an open-winged beauty.

The woman turned suddenly and Charlotte blushed, embarrassed to have been caught out staring at her. She smiled, and the woman smiled back.

"Your first?" she said, nodding at Charlotte's bump.

"Yes."

"How far along are you?"

"Twenty-nine weeks."

"Ah, that's a nice time, I seem to remember. I'd stopped riding my bike by then and was walking everywhere. Just me and him." She pointed to the little boy. "It was a great bonding experience." Her voice switched captivatingly between a lilting South West burr and a clipped London accent.

"Mummy! Mumm*eeeee*!" The child held up his arms and she lifted him onto her lap. Gurgling happily, he turned to face her and patted his hands on her cheeks.

Charlotte watched as the woman laughed and pulled the baby close, rocking him back and forth. It was a perfectly normal action and one that millions of mothers throughout the world carried out countless times every day but in Charlotte's highly emotional state, it was the trigger for more spontaneous tears.

"Oh, are you okay?" the woman called across to her.

"Oh, I'm so sorry! How embarrassing! Yes, I'm fine. It's my hormones. They've been catching me out for a couple of weeks now." Charlotte retrieved Nathan's handkerchief from up her sleeve and wiped her eyes. "I'm actually quite rational, usually!" She blew her nose and grinned.

"No need to apologise," sympathised the woman. "I spent almost five weeks in floods of tears one minute and screaming blue murder at Owen the next." She nodded at the man standing close by and he turned, a half-smile on his lips.

"Ah, yes, but I was prepared for every eventuality so I took it all in my stride," he said. "Plenty of earplugs and camomile tea to maintain the serenity levels."

The woman laughed. "He was so brilliant. If I'd been him, I think I would have scared me off. Every minute was worth it, though. This little fella makes up for all of it. Don't you, Zac?" She bounced her son on her knees and he squealed with gurgling baby laughter. She turned back to Charlotte. "Where are you off to?"

"London."

"Hey! Us, too. You're not going for the Internat Tat Awards, by any chance, are you?"

"The what?"

"The International Tattoo Artist of the Year Awards." The woman laughed. "That's a bit of a mouthful, though, so we call it the Internat Tat Awards. It's a lot easier!" She nodded to the crowds. "Quite a lot of people are going."

"Ah, I see—that explains all the tattoos." Charlotte smiled. "Anyway, to answer your question, no, we're not going for the awards. We're on our belated honeymoon."

"Oh, congratulations! Where are you staying?
"At The Milestone."

The woman gave a low whistle of approval. "Very nice—fabulous hotel. We might even bump into each other—our place is on the next street back. It's close to where the awards ceremony's being held and it saves on hotel bills. There's a crowd of us, see." She gestured to the group of people around her. "And little Zac, of course." She tickled his bare feet and he gave a joyful squeal.

"We're all clients of the tattooist who's up for the award," the woman explained, upon seeing Charlotte's blank look. "Well, almost all of us. That's him over there—Frankie Ingram—talking to my sister, Amy."

Charlotte followed the woman's pointing finger to see a short, muscular man in a t-shirt and ripped jeans, a denim jacket tied loosely around his hips and a slouchy beanie hat pulled down over his head. A large brightly-coloured tattoo of a skull and crossbones adorned his thick neck, which he constantly scratched throughout his conversation with a young woman whose butter-blonde hair fell in an immaculate sheet over her shoulders. Charlotte noticed that when he said something which made her laugh, she touched his heavily tattooed bicep lightly and smiled adoringly.

"Yeah, so anyway, " the woman continued, "he's been nominated for the past four years and come second every time but this year, we're sure that trophy has his name on it. We always travel up to support him, although I missed the actual ceremony last year because Zac was only six months old. It's pretty major—nominees from all over the world travel to London especially for it."

The woman moved her baby from one leg to the other before sticking out her hand. "I'm Penny, by the way."

"Nice to meet you. I'm Charlotte," she said, pushing herself up from her suitcase to shake hands. "And who knows, maybe we *will* bump into each other."

As she pulled her hand back, the toddler grabbed hold of her thumb and grinned up at her. Even though his chin was covered in dribble he was the cutest thing, and enough to prompt the tears to come spilling out again before she had a chance to keep them in check.

"Oh, dear...sorry."

Nathan reappeared with a trolley, to find Charlotte reaching for his handkerchief again.

"Everything alright?"

"We were just talking about how your hormones can mess you up. She's a little emotional," explained Penny.

"You *could* say that." Nathan smiled as he loaded the cases onto the trolley. "But she was pretty emotional *before* the baby, so it's not altogether unexpected." He grinned. "Anyway, we must get these cases checked in, so we'd better make a move."

"Good luck with the rest of your pregnancy, Charlotte," said Penny, taking her baby's hand and waving it up and down. "Say bye-bye, Zac." The little boy bounced on chubby legs and sent Charlotte a beaming smile and a gurgly baby chuckle.

She tried to smile back at him, but her hormones had other ideas.

As she dissolved into another heap of tears, Nathan grinned and pulled her into a hug, dropping a kiss on top of her head. "Come on. Let's go and get rid of these cases and find somewhere to have a cup of tea."

ooooooo

In the departure lounge, Charlotte couldn't concentrate on her book. Beside her, Nathan was engrossed in the newspaper.

"I'm going to get a packet of mints and some more tissues. I won't be long. You want anything?"

"No, thanks, but can you get the super-strong mints instead of those insipid spearmint ones?"

"But I like the insipid spearmint ones!"

"Yeah...I don't, though." He winked at her over the top of his paper, which Charlotte took great pleasure in giving a hard flick.

"I won't be long. Save my seat for me."

In the duty-free shop, she picked up four packets of mints—two spearmint and two super-strong. On the way back to her seat, she saw Penny and the rest of her travelling companions in the departure lounge café. Their table was loaded with babies' bottles, nappies, and the mountain of other paraphernalia which seemed to accompany parents with young children wherever they went.

Completely oblivious to her, they were gabbing excitedly as they enjoyed the start of their holiday.

"Here, these are for you." She handed Nathan his mints over the top of his newspaper.

"For *me*? Why, thank you. What an unexpected treat." He opened a packet immediately and popped one into his mouth.

She kissed him on the cheek and settled back for a relaxing session of people-watching.

As she scanned the travellers milling around, her gaze went back to the nearby café and the group of friends.

Penny—pale-skinned with a dusting of freckles across the bridge of her aquiline nose—was deep in conversation with Owen, her fair head close to his dark one.

The woman she'd pointed out as her sister was tucking into a tub of chocolate ice cream, still debating with Frankie, the tattooist, her eyes fixed firmly on him as she spoke and ate simultaneously. He pulled a face and reached forward as if to ruffle her perfect hair, but she dodged out of reach and rapped him on the nose with her ice-cream spoon, prompting a fit of giggles.

"Ow! You could have broken my nose, you numpty!" said Frankie. "In case you'd forgotten, I *may* have to make a very public appearance this week and I'd rather keep my nose in the *middle* of my face, if it's all the same to you."

Still laughing, but seemingly contrite, the woman gave him a hug and held her ice cream tub against the bridge of his nose to soothe the bump.

Grinning at their antics, Charlotte moved her gaze to the three people at the end of the table.

A woman wearing a short tunic dress, ballet slippers, a cowboy hat atop her long, chestnut waves, and sporting a large tattoo of a bunch of purple orchids on her calf was throwing baby Zac into the air, his giggles reverberating around the departure lounge

It occurred to Charlotte that, despite the gurgling baby, the woman looked a little uptight. She wondered if the man sitting beside her was her husband. He looked vaguely familiar, but she couldn't place him. Engrossed in a broadsheet, he shook the paper out in front of him, immediately becoming an unwitting, and, evidently, unwilling, partner in little Zac's latest game of grabbing at the pages to reveal the man's face for a game of peek-a-boo.

As the man turned away from the little boy with barely concealed irritation, he leaned over and spoke quietly to the young man sitting beside him. Seconds later, they'd changed places, leaving the man to read his newspaper in peace and the younger man to deal with little Zac.

Charlotte noticed the immediate change in the woman's demeanour as she became noticeably relaxed. She guessed her to be in her late thirties, or thereabouts, and the older man anywhere between his mid-fifties and mid-sixties. Although they'd sat together, there was no other evidence of closeness, and Charlotte observed a palpable detachment between them. Together—but not quite.

"I'm going to check the board." Nathan interrupted her thoughts. "And if there's no gate number, I'm going for a quick walk. My backside's gone to sleep." He winced as he stood up and stretched out his back before folding his newspaper and handing it to the woman in the next seat, who accepted it with a smile.

As he went off in search of gate information, Charlotte turned her attention back to the group of friends.

Hamburgers, Homicide and a Honeymoon

Frankie had joined in the game of peek-a-boo now, pulling his beanie hat down over his eyes and then pulling it up again to boo Zac, making him squeal with delight. He took the hat off after a while and fanned his face with it and, as he bent to retrieve his backpack from under the table, Charlotte did a double-take.

The back of his shaved head was a canvas for a tattoo of a full-sized face, complete with piercing green eyes surrounded by bloodshot whites and thin lips curled sneeringly over teeth bared in a contemptuous snarl.

"Look at that guy's tattoo," she whispered to Nathan, when he came back. "That's so creepy."

"Bloody hell. Brings a whole new meaning to the phrase 'eyes in the back of your head', doesn't it? Hey… isn't that… I'm sure it is…" Nathan craned his neck and squinted. "Yes, it's definitely him."

"It's definitely who?" Charlotte followed his gaze.

"Aidan Pitt. The guy reading the paper is Aidan Pitt."

Charlotte suddenly realised why he'd looked familiar. Back in St. Eves, Aidan Pitt was a minor celebrity.

Not that celebrities were an unusual occurrence in St. Eves. Quite often you couldn't walk down the street without tripping over one who was holidaying at their weekend retreat. Actors, rock stars, politicians and TV personalities were flocking to put down roots in the town, some arriving with an entourage but others preferring to come and go, almost unnoticed and without any fuss. Aidan Pitt was certainly one of the more guarded.

A successful property tycoon, his considerable fortune had been significantly enhanced when he'd sold his lucrative construction company and made a series of incredibly impressive killings on the stock market by taking calculated risks while others were being overly-cautious.

Four years ago, before taking early retirement and relocating to St. Eves, he'd caused a sensation when he'd refused to renew his contract as business adviser on the prime-time financial affairs TV programme, *Your Money in Our Hands*.

With his no-nonsense approach and shrewd eye for business, he had helped thousands of viewers to bring their financial problems under control, gaining an army of fans along the way.

However, apart from the flurry of media interest pre and post his arrival in the town, he appeared to have shunned any subsequent attention. However, that hadn't stopped a devoted following of admirers from gaining in numbers since his arrival—a group of mainly middle-aged women who called themselves 'The Pittettes'.

Charlotte recalled there'd been a minor hullabaloo when he'd moved into a listed building on the edge of St. Eves but, as there'd been more serious matters on her mind at the time—a murder in the town that she'd become involved in helping to solve, for one—she'd paid little attention to it.

She did recall hearing, though, that when he'd arrived he'd brought his ex-programme researcher with him, leaving behind an estranged wife with whom he'd had no contact for years. When his divorce had come through six months later on the grounds of irreconcilable differences, he'd married his ex-programme researcher and made Ruby Danvers the current Mrs Pitt.

"Oh, right. I wondered why he looked familiar. So is that his wife, then? The woman with the dark hair?"

"I'm not sure," said Nathan. "It might be—I don't think I've ever seen her before."

A crackle over the loudspeaker heralded the announcement they'd been waiting for.

"This is an announcement for all passengers on flight UKLG421 to London Gatwick. At this time, we are inviting those passengers with small children, any passengers requiring special assistance, and passengers who are eligible for rapid boarding, to approach the gate. Please have your boarding pass and identification ready for inspection. Boarding of all remaining passengers will begin in approximately ten minutes' time. Thank you."

ooooooo

The hotel was grand, but not in the slightest bit pretentious.

Elegant, comfortable, and luxurious, it was the perfect place to spend a honeymoon. Charlotte had felt herself relax immediately as she'd set foot on the canopied entrance walkway and stepped into the sumptuous foyer.

As Nathan reclined on the bed, head resting in clasped fingers, Charlotte read off a lengthy 'To Do' list.

"So, that's Buckingham Palace, The Changing of the Guards, Trooping the Colour—I'm so happy we're here for the Queen's birthday—Harvey Nichols, Oxford Street, The Marylebone Farmers Market, The Princess Di memorial fountain and the Peter Pan statue in Hyde Park, a boat trip along the Thames, lunch on one of those boat restaurants along Regents Canal, a sightseeing tour on an open-topped bus, The London Eye, Madame Tussauds,

and St. Martin's theatre. Oh, and tea at The Ritz."
Charlotte tapped her pen against her teeth. "Yes, I think that's everything."

Nathan opened an eye and arched a brow. "I see. Sure you haven't missed anything off?"

Charlotte's reviewed her list. "Ooh yes—all the museums and lunch at Kensington Palace."

Nathan shook his head. "You do realise we're only here for two weeks?"

"Course I do. Why?"

"Because you should be relaxing, and that itinerary sounds anything but."

Charlotte flopped down on the bed. "Listen, you old grump." She poked Nathan in the ribs with her pen. "I'm not ill—I'm pregnant. I just want to make the most of being here, and what better way to do that than sightseeing?"

She grinned. "And you'd better get used to it because I'm going to buy a Union Jack t-shirt and a hat with 'I Love London' written on the front. While we're here, I'm a tourist and I'm going to make the most of it. This is our capital city, Nathan, and it's fantastic. I want to see everything I can." She took his hand and dragged him onto the Juliet balcony. "Just look at it."

Everywhere they looked was architecture from centuries gone by, and sights that Charlotte couldn't wait to visit. Not far away was the green dome of Madame Tussauds waxwork museum, the shimmering Serpentine River slithering its way through the green banks of Hyde Park, and the London Eye slowly turning, each of its pods filled with tourists eager for their bird's-eye view of the capital city in all its glory.

As if to reinforce Charlotte's resolve, a red double-decker bus drove past and she suddenly felt wildly patriotic.

"So, are you coming with me on this adventure or would you rather stay here and watch the shopping channel?" Her eyes twinkled mischievously. When she put her mind to it, she could sweet-talk Nathan into doing anything she wanted.

Nathan rolled his eyes. "Okay, Mrs Costello. You win."

ooooooo

Almost a week into their honeymoon, in the hotel restaurant with its spacious white marble interior adorned with tasteful art, leafy palms, and a bevy of claret-waistcoated attentive servers for whom nothing was too much trouble, Charlotte added four kisses to the postcard she'd just written to Jess and Laura and stuck a stamp onto the top right-hand corner.

A waiter holding aloft two plates, each bearing a piping hot selection from the breakfast menu, arrived at the table.

"Scrambled eggs on maple syrup French toast, with cheddar cheese, mushrooms, and a side order of pickled baby beetroot for you, Madam and, for you, Sir, our full English breakfast. And would you care for more tea and coffee?"

"Tea, please," said Charlotte before sinking her teeth into a deep burgundy pickle. She was grateful that whatever her craving, the hotel kitchen catered to her bizarre breakfast requests without quibble. She took her list out of her pocket and laid it on the table. "So, how about Madame Tussauds after breakfast and then Hyde

Park? I can't wait to see the Princess Diana Memorial Fountain. That okay with you?"

Nathan nodded. "Suits me. When we're ready for lunch we can grab a couple of sandwiches from the deli on the corner and eat them in the park, if you like?"

"Deal!" Charlotte crossed two more items off her list and mopped up a pool of maple syrup from her plate with a triangle of French toast. "I love it when a plan comes together!"

ooooooo

The memorial, fashioned from Cornish granite, was just as beautiful as Charlotte had imagined it to be and, after a busy morning of sightseeing, she and Nathan relaxed in deck chairs at the edge of the Serpentine River in Hyde Park.

It was a glorious day and, all around, visitors to the park were taking advantage of the good weather: sunbathers reclined on the warm grass, joggers pounded the footpaths, families ambled alongside the river, and gaggles of gossiping young nannies commandeered park benches, their gleeful charges delighted to be free from the confines of their pushchairs. Everyone seemed to be taking the opportunity to appreciate the park.

Everyone apart from a smartly dressed man, fixated on his phone and completely oblivious to his beautiful surroundings.

Nathan's roast beef and mustard sandwich came to a halt mid-way to his mouth. "Look, it's Aidan Pitt."

Charlotte turned. "So it is. He looks awfully serious. Wonder what he's up to?"

Nathan laughed. "What do you mean you 'wonder what he's up to'? He's on his phone, is what he's up to. You've been involved in too many murders, that's your problem—you think everyone's up to no good these days. You're worse than me."

Charlotte was about to answer when a young woman on a bicycle pulled up alongside Aidan. Strands of blonde hair escaped from underneath the baseball cap she wore and Charlotte immediately recognised her as being Penny, the woman she'd spoken to at the airport.

The couple spoke quietly for a while before the conversation appeared to become heated. It was impossible to hear what was being said but Penny as clearly upset by something. When her raised voice attracted glances from passers-by, she shook Aidan's hand from her shoulder and cycled off.

"Wonder what that was all about?" Charlotte frowned as Aidan strode away.

Nathan shrugged a shoulder and pushed an escaping piece of roast beef back into his mouth. "Who knows? Lovers' tiff, maybe?"

"D'you think so? He's married, though."

"And? Married people have affairs all the time—you don't know *what* might be going on." Nathan washed down the last bite of his sandwich with a swig of mineral water and leaned back in his deckchair. "I'm just glad that, whatever it is, I don't have to analyse anything anyone says or does because, for once, it's absolutely none of my business."

As Charlotte watched Aidan disappear out of sight, a familiar niggling worry overwhelmed her. As she tilted her face to the sun, she hoped her instincts were wrong.

ooooooo

Charlotte was about to cross a long-time ambition off her list.

After an early dinner at a popular local restaurant, they were off to St. Martin's theatre to see Agatha Christie's, *The Mousetrap*.

"You know they ask the audience to keep whodunit a secret?" she said as she attempted to pick up a Chinese pork dumpling with chopsticks.

"Will you *please* let me help you?" said Nathan. "Or why don't you just use a knife and fork? You're not going to get anything to eat at this rate—I can't bear to watch for much longer."

"No, thank you and I'm determined to master these flippin' things, so I won't be resorting to cutlery. I nearly had it then…c'mere, you little…ah, got it! See, I told you I'd get the hang—oops!" Charlotte froze as she lost her grip on the dumpling and it catapulted through the air, towards an elderly woman who looked as though she'd come straight from the hairdresser.

"*Got it!*" a voice called out and, from nowhere, a figure jumped and caught the wayward dumpling mid-flight, to a ripple of applause.

Immediately, Charlotte knew who it was. Who else had a tattoo of a face on the back of their head?

"Frankie Ingram—at your service." The grinning tattoo artist from the airport, placed the dumpling on the table in front of Charlotte. "I believe this is yours?"

"Thank you. I'm very embarrassed and incredibly grateful." Charlotte put down her chopsticks and picked up her knife and fork immediately. "Thank goodness you were here to catch it. It was heading straight for that woman's shampoo and set."

"You're welcome. I knew all that rugby training would come in handy sooner or later. Actually, we were just wondering if it was you." He pointed to a table a little way behind them, at which sat Penny and the rest of the group from the airport.

"Hi!" Penny waved frantically. "See, I told you we'd bump into each other! You want to join us? Owen's cousin's looking after Zac until tomorrow so we're making the most of our night off!"

"Thanks, but we're off to the theatre in a while. We've got tickets for *The Mousetrap*—I can't tell you how long I've wanted to see that play. Nathan reckons he'll have the murderer figured out during the first act, but I'm not so sure he'll be able to second-guess Agatha!"

Penny laughed. "Well, I won't tell you whodunit but I bet you'll never guess. Anyway, as we've bumped into you, what better time to ask if you'd like to come to a small party we're having tomorrow afternoon? Actually, it's a victory party for Frankie—we're so sure he's going to win big at the awards tonight, it's a good excuse for a celebration. If you'd like to come along, we'd love to see you. And you won't have far to go because we're in the street just behind your hotel—number 196. If you're interested, just turn up any time after midday and before six. The weather's going to be great so Owen's doing a barbecue—come along if you can, it'll be fun.

"Oh, and we'll have the hot tub going for the first time this year if you want to get in or dangle your legs over the side. We keep loads of spare swimsuits and swimming shorts at the house if you haven't brought anything with you and you'd like to borrow something."

Charlotte looked at Nathan and nodded. "Okay, we'll see how we're fixed. Number 196, did you say?"

"Yeah. It's the red-brick house with the black and white eaves and the post-box outside that says 'Baker'—you can't miss it. I hope you can make it."

"Okay, maybe see you tomorrow. Thanks for the invite. We'll leave you to finish your meal in peace. Good luck for tonight, Frankie, and thanks for the save."

The young man made a Victory sign before expertly manipulating a piece of Kung Po Chicken into his mouth with his chopsticks.

ooooooo

"Bet you didn't see that coming, did you, Inspector Clouseau?"

"Er, I think I prefer Inspector Poirot, if you don't mind. And no, I didn't. I must be losing my touch." Nathan settled Charlotte's jacket around her shoulders as they made their way out of the theatre.

"Nice of Penny to invite us to her party. They seem like nice people, don't you think?"

"Yeah, they seem harmless enough. Do you want to go?"

Charlotte allowed herself a secret smile. It wasn't often that Nathan welcomed the company of strangers so readily. Years of being a policeman had made him instinctively wary but, over the past few days, Charlotte had seen a new side of him and she loved that he was so relaxed.

"We can pop in for a while, I suppose. I mean, she's been good enough to invite us so the least we can do is show our faces—we don't have to stay for long if we don't want to. By the way, did you notice that Aidan

Pitt bloke at the table? He looked really grumpy—and he was crotchety at the airport, too. I wondered if perhaps he doesn't like the thought of strangers joining their little group. D'you know what I mean? He might feel uncomfortable with us being there, what with him being a minor celebrity and all."

Nathan shook his head. "No, I didn't notice he was grumpy but we're not all Pollyannas, you know. Just because someone doesn't have an ear-to-ear grin 24/7 doesn't mean there's something wrong with them. Maybe he was tired, or fed up? Who knows? And if he had an issue with being among strangers, I doubt he'd have come all the way to London for a tattoo awards ceremony."

"Maybe he's fed up because of the argument we saw him having with Penny?" said Charlotte, drumming her fingers against her chin.

Nathan rolled his eyes. "Or maybe we should completely forget about Aidan Pitt and his mood swings? And, incidentally, you've got that faraway look in your eyes. You know, the one you always get before you start meddling in something that's none of your business."

"What *look*? I don't have 'a faraway look,'" said Charlotte indignantly. "But if I *did*, why d'you suppose that is? I'll tell you why—it's because St. Eves has become the UK's flippin' murder hotspot over the past few years and I've had to become accustomed to solving mysteries."

"Actually," said Nathan, putting an arm around her and kissing the top of her head, "you haven't *had* to do anything, but that hasn't stopped you from turning into the local amateur sleuth who won't rest until justice is done, tearing around town on that bicycle of yours and channelling your inner Ms Marple."

Charlotte opened her mouth to retort but closed it again. "It's Miss, not Ms… and I suppose I am a bit like that, aren't I?"

"Yes, you are, but I wouldn't change you for anything." Nathan pulled her a little closer. "Tell you what, how about we go back to the hotel, see if that group that's supposed to be performing tonight is any good and then have a nightcap before turning in?"

"Good idea." Charlotte pulled her jacket tightly around her and put all thoughts of Aidan Pitt from her mind. "I could murder a strawberry sherbet cocktail and a pickled egg!"

Chapter 2

Nathan pressed the buzzer on the panel next to the navy-blue front door. A crackling preceded a man's voice, with music and laughter in the background. "Hi, it's Charlotte and Nathan Costello. Penny invited us."

"Oh, right. Hang on." They heard the man put his hand over the receiver and call out to Penny. Seconds later, he was back. "Okay. Someone'll be out in a sec."

"If only more people were as vigilant about letting people into their homes, there'd be a lot less crime." Nathan took off his sunglasses and put them in his shirt pocket. "People like this are an asset to any neighbourhood—I just wish everyone was as cautious."

"Yes, Detective Chief Inspector." Charlotte turned to her husband and smiled sweetly. "But please promise me you won't make that a subject for conversation this afternoon. This is a party, not The Resident of the Year Awards."

Nathan's retort was cut short as the front door was flung open by Frankie—tattooist and dumpling-catcher extraordinaire—a winner's sash draped around his neck and a large, Champagne-filled silver trophy in his hand from which he was drinking liberally. His wide smile was the antithesis of the snarling face on the back of his head and it was obvious there was cause to celebrate.

"I take it congratulations are in order?" Nathan said, shaking Frankie's hand.

"Certainly are. First place, no less! I'm chuffed to bits. Anyway, come in. Come in and join the party." He led the way through the spacious, black and white tiled entrance hall and into the living room.

"Oh my, what a gorgeous house. I bet those are all original features." Charlotte pointed at the ceiling roses, the cornicing, and the large bay windows with stained glass panels.

"Yeah, they are. Wait till you see the garden." Frankie led them outside to where the guests were congregated on and around a tiled patio, either reclining on loungers or sitting in the shade of swinging chairs.

Penny and Amy's London home was a handsome Edwardian house. Their childhood home, frequented so rarely in recent times since the family had moved away from London, had become theirs when their parents had handed the keys to their eldest daughter six years previously and told her to share it fairly with her younger sister.

Since then, it had become a welcome bolthole for the sisters and their friends and, over the years, it had proved its worth, not only as the ideal party venue, but also as a haven of peaceful solitude.

Large rooms with high ceilings and solid walls had been soundproofed by the sisters to allow their parties to go on until dawn without disturbing the neighbours. In the warmer weather, gatherings spilled out into the established garden, complete with fruit trees, country garden shrubs and herbs, and a hot tub big enough for ten situated in the shadow of an ornate pergola.

"Charlotte! You made it!" Penny greeted her, arms outstretched.

"We did. Thanks for inviting us. I'm not sure I've introduced my husband yet? This is—"

"DCI Nathan Costello." Penny finished Charlotte's sentence as she shook Nathan's hand. "Hi, nice to meet you. I thought I recognised you at the airport but Aidan confirmed it was you after we saw you in the restaurant yesterday. It's not always easy to place people when you see them out of their usual environment, is it? Anyway, let me introduce you to everyone.

"This is my boyfriend, Owen; our friends, Ruby and her husband, Aidan; and Aidan's assistant, Eddie. And over there," she pointed to a couple playing cricket with little Zac, "are Owen's cousin, Danny, and his wife, Susan, who live just around the corner and who are the *best* babysitters. And that's my sister, Amy, over there and you already know Frankie, our triumphant tattoo artist, who's in rather a celebratory mood, as you can see!"

As Frankie danced on the grass with Amy, his sash now draped around both of them, Charlotte marvelled at the tattoos on the young woman's body. Two snakes, one of fire and one of ice, entwined and reached up her right side from her ankle to the top of her thigh; another of a peacock, its tail feathers spreading across her back and shoulders; and a third of a fallen angel on her forearm. Each one was a work of art on skin.

"They're wonderful, aren't they?" said Penny. "They're what won Frankie the prize—Amy's his model, you see."

"Oh, I see. Well, I can see how they would have won him first prize—they're incredible. I don't have any myself—too scared of needles—but I can appreciate them on other people. I've never seen one like Frankie's got on the back of his head before, though!"

"Oh, you mean Freddy?" Penny smiled. "That's what Frankie calls it. Yes, it's unusual, isn't it? That's Amy's work—she's been training to become a tattooist for a while. Personally, I think Frankie was crazy to let her loose on his head—I mean, if she'd messed it up, he would have been wearing a hat for an awfully long time but, thankfully, the end result was pretty good." She looked at her watch.

"Well, I expect you'd like a drink? If you tell Eddie what you'd like, he'll make up whatever you want." Penny gave Charlotte's arm a friendly squeeze. "Right, Owen, come and help me bring the stuff for the barbecue, will you?"

Introductions over, Aidan Pitt made a point of coming over to shake Nathan's hand and engaging him in conversation. Although he was pleasant enough, Charlotte got the distinct impression that he was really only interested in talking to Nathan so, when the conversation turned to politics, she took the opportunity to slink off in search of a more light-hearted discussion.

She made her way over to Ruby Pitt who was sitting alone on a large bench swing, a large glass of wine in her hand and the brim of a sizeable straw hat covering half her face.

"Hi. Do you mind if I share the seat with you?"

Ruby pulled back her hat to reveal round sunglasses with pink-mirrored lenses, and smiled. "Not at all. Come and take the weight off your feet. When's your baby due?"

"August 11th and it can't come soon enough." Charlotte manoeuvred herself onto the bench, not entirely convinced that she wouldn't topple out of it out on one of its backward swings. "It's not easy getting on one of these, is it? Maybe I'd be better off in one of the basket chairs."

Ruby rocked the swing gently with her foot. "Don't worry, you'll be fine—it's a strange sensation at first but you'll get used to it. It's just like being on a swing when you were a kid but you can't hold on with both hands. We'll chat—it'll take your mind off falling on your backside!" She sipped her wine. "So, this is your first baby, I take it? Do you know if it's going to be a boy or a girl?"

Charlotte shook her head. "No, we want it to be a surprise. We think it's better that way. Do you have any children?" It was a perfectly innocent question but—from Ruby's reaction—was one Charlotte wished she hadn't asked immediately it had left her lips.

Ruby visibly tensed, her smile forced and her voice tight. "No. We don't. I wanted them after we got married but Aidan was always too busy. You've heard the phrase 'married to the job?' Yeah, well, I reckon Aidan must have been the inspiration behind it. Even though he's been retired for ages, he hardly ever has any free time. He's either on the phone to a business associate, or looking for the next big thing to put his money into. He was a total workaholic when I met him and he's a total workaholic now. Silly me for thinking that early retirement would mean we'd have the time to concentrate on raising a family."

Her tinkly laugh didn't quite hide the bitter edge to her voice. "He gave me this, though." She held out her hand and the sunlight caught the huge rock in her engagement ring, casting rainbows all around. "He seemed to think it would make up for the absence of a baby." She laughed again, a hint of melancholy replacing the bitterness. "Anyway, there's still time but not much. I'm 43 and Aidan's 61. Tick-tock, if you know what I mean." She raised her glass before downing the contents in one and refilling it immediately.

"Are you going in the hot tub?" Charlotte was as keen to change the subject as she was for someone else to join them. As pleasant as Ruby was, the last thing Charlotte wanted was to be stuck alone in the company of an inebriated woman who was in charge of how high the chair would swing.

"Yes, I'm definitely going in," said Ruby, pulling her long hair up into a ponytail. "We're late using it this year—usually, it's the first thing we get set up but, when we arrived, Zac and Penny went down with some sort of 24-hour stomach bug, then Owen got it and then me, Amy, and Eddie. Frankie and Aidan were the only ones who managed to avoid it but Frankie was too wound up thinking about the awards to be bothered with the hot tub. And Aidan was too busy on the phone to his investment broker." She rolled her eyes. "What about you?"

"No, I don't think I'd better risk it," said Charlotte. "I'm not bothered, though—as long as I've got a cold drink and someone to chat to, I'll be happy. Ah, speaking of drinks, here comes Eddie with mine." She took the non-alcoholic cocktail she'd asked for, grateful for a brief respite from a potentially draining conversation with Ruby.

"Here you are—one mango, passionfruit, and strawberry fizz," said Eddie, pushing his sunglasses up onto his head. "You've got the café on the marina, haven't you? *Charlotte's Plaice*—that's it, isn't it?"

"Yes, that's right. Have you been in?"

"He nodded. "It was a while ago, though."

Charlotte was embarrassed that she didn't recognise him and she knew she definitely would have if she'd met him. Although quite unremarkable-looking, Eddie had the biggest dimples she'd ever seen and towered above her at well over six foot tall. "I'm sorry, I could lie and tell you that I remember but I don't. I'm in the kitchen most of the time, you see, so I don't see half the customers. If you come in again, make a point of saying hello, won't you?"

Eddie nodded. "I definitely will. I don't come down to the marina much—usually too busy during the day with work—but I took my mum there one day a couple of years ago for Sunday lunch when Aidan and Ruby went to Paris for a long weekend. She loves marinas."

"You're right about it being a 'long weekend'—it was the longest weekend of my life," said Ruby. "We were only there for three days and it rained cats and dogs from the minute we arrived to the minute we left. Aidan spent most of the time on his laptop talking to anyone but me, and I spent most of mine in the hotel shop and ordering room service. The City of Love? Hmpf, not for us, it wasn't. Was it, Aidan? *Aidan!*" When there was no response forthcoming from her husband, she set about opening another bottle of wine, muttering under her breath.

Charlotte shaded her eyes and looked over to Aidan who was still deep in conversation with Nathan.

What an ignorant pig. I could be doing him a disservice but, as far as first impressions go, he hasn't made a very good one with me.

"Anyway," Eddie continued. "It was a fantastic lunch—my Mum raved about your Yorkshire puddings for ages afterwards!"

Charlotte chuckled. "Good, I'm glad she enjoyed it. I hope you'll be able to bring her again. Perhaps I could meet her next time?"

Their conversation came to a halt as Owen and Penny reappeared, their arms laden with trays of meat, fish and vegetables for the barbecue.

"Right, you lot—food'll be about an hour and I hope you're hungry because there's a lot of it." Owen prodded the coals, and the embers glowed as they spluttered and spat. "As soon as this food's done, there's a space in that hot tub with my name on it," he said, dodging a wayward fragment of lava-hot coal as it whistled past his ear.

"Owen, you're going to have someone's eye out if you don't leave those flippin' coals alone!" Penny held out an ice cold bottle of beer with a wedge of lime sticking out of the neck. "Come and sit down and wait for them to turn white, for goodness' sake."

She shook her head. "Honestly, he's like this every time we have a barbecue," she said to Charlotte. "He doesn't have the patience to wait until the coals are hot enough and then the meat doesn't cook properly. Remember last year, Rube?"

Ruby rolled her eyes. "Oh yeah, I'd forgotten about that. All the food was burnt on the outside and completely raw on the inside. My burger was positively mooing, it was so rare."

"Don't you mean raw?" Penny pulled a face.

"Well, yes, that, too."

"Ha-ha, very amusing. Glad you all found it so entertaining," said Owen, checking the coals again.

"'Scuse me. Sorry to interrupt." Penny's sister, Amy, came running over. "Pen, can I have a word? Over here."

The sisters stepped away as Ruby began to give a full-blown account of the previous year's barbecue. Charlotte listened with one ear—the other one was earwigging on Amy and Penny's conversation.

"Can I borrow your swimsuit?" said Amy. "The one with the high neck?"

"What, the yellow one?"

"No, the green halter-neck one with the sunflowers on it."

"Oh, right," said Penny. "Yeah, if you want. It's in the top drawer in the bedroom."

The young woman ran off, with Frankie following close behind.

"So, you said you all come to support Frankie every year. Are you all clients of his?" asked Charlotte as Penny re-joined them.

"We're not." Owen's cousin, Danny, and his wife came over to join them with Zac, who was pink-faced and puffing after his game of cricket. "But you probably guessed that anyway, seeing as we live 300 miles away from his tattoo shop!"

"And Aidan's not, either." Ruby took off her sunglasses and lowered her voice. "To be honest, I don't really know why he's here. Not only does he not have any tattoos, but he's never shown any interest in the awards before. I've no idea why he suddenly decided to come along. When I asked him why, he said he wanted a change of scenery. I mean, I love him to death but having him here is a bit like having the headmaster looking over your shoulder while you're at a school disco."

Owen returned, crunching on an ice cube and rubbing his forehead to counteract the brain freeze. "It's all very well Aidan wanting a change of scene," he said, quietly, joining in the conversation, "but it's completely ruined Eddie's trip. He only found out Aidan was coming the day before we travelled—he told him to get him on the same flight as the rest of us. I mean, Eddie's a good friend of Frankie's, so he'd have liked to celebrate with him, wouldn't you mate?"

Eddie shrugged. "It's okay. I don't mind—I haven't had to do much work since I've been here. I just have to make sure I lay off the booze in case Aidan decides he needs me to do something."

"Yes, my point exactly," said Owen as he handed out cold beers, missing Eddie out. "You can't let your hair down while the boss is here, can you?" He turned to Ruby. "You know I've nothing against Aidan, Rube, but he doesn't even seem to be enjoying himself. I just don't understa—"

"Oh look, here come Aidan and Nathan," said Penny, her voice deliberately raised in an attempt to shut Owen up. "And their bottles are empty. Give them a beer, will you, love?"

"When can we get in the hot tub?" said Eddie. "It's ready, right?"

"Yep, it's ready when you are." Penny slathered sun tan lotion onto her shoulders and arms. "But I bet you won't get in there before Amy." She turned to Charlotte. "I love her to bits but she's *such* an exhibitionist and *so* competitive. She always has to be the first one in the tub."

Owen rolled his eyes and tapped the neck of his beer bottle against Nathan's and Aidan's. "Yeah, usually in the tiniest bikini you've ever seen. Bloody hell! D'you remember last year? It was like four postage stamps held together with string. If this year's version is any smaller than that, someone had better cover my eyes. Or resuscitate me."

Penny swiped at him good-humouredly with a salad server. "Oh, be quiet and get on with the barbecue. You'd better get some of that stuff cooking or we'll be eating at midnight at this rate. And I'm sorry to disappoint you, but Amy won't be wearing quite such a revealing swimsuit today."

Ruby raised an eyebrow. "Really? Well, that'll be a first!" She glanced at Charlotte. "She's got the most fabulous figure—I don't blame her for showing it off—so I can't imagine why she wants to cover up."

Charlotte nodded and smiled, and was pondering the reason for Amy's sudden attack of inhibition, when a ring on the doorbell interrupted her thoughts.

"Wonder who that can be?" Penny put down her drink and padded inside, reappearing soon afterwards with a small, bespectacled woman with a ramrod straight back, a twin set, a tweed skirt, and a pair of sturdy brogues.

A wild thatch of bleached hair with dark roots made her small head seem considerably larger than it actually was, and the overall effect of a slightly eccentric senior citizen was completed by a large bunch of keys strung around her neck and a tabby kitten under her arm.

"Afternoon, Elsie." Owen raised his bottle to the woman, who sniffed and barely acknowledged him.

"As I was just saying to Penny," said the woman, peering through her thick lenses, one of her light-blue irises completely obscured by a cataract's milky white haze. "I hope you're not going to be making any noise because I've got my granddaughter staying with me and if she gets woken up from her afternoon nap by your shenanigans, I won't be best pleased. It takes an age to get her to sleep, doesn't it, Idris, darling." The cat purred loudly as she scratched it under the chin.

"We'll be as quiet as we can, Elsie, but we're celebrating so we can't promise there'll be no noise at all. I mean," Owen looked at his watch, "it's only half-past one, not the middle of the night."

"I don't see why you can't have your party indoors—then you wouldn't disturb anyone at all. Wasn't that the sole reason for having the place soundproofed?"

"Well, yes, that's true," Owen reasoned, "but if we did, you'd have to come back in an hour and give us all a good basting because we'd cook if we stayed inside today with the doors shut—it must be at least 80 degrees out here so it'd be like a furnace in there."

"And then there's the barbecue, Elsie." Penny threw her curmudgeonly neighbour a benevolent smile. "We couldn't take *that* inside. Or the hot tub."

"Hmpf, oh yes. The *hot tub*." Elsie uttered the words as if she found them highly offensive. "Why anyone needs a communal bathtub outside is beyond me—all that cavorting around half-naked in broad daylight. And as for that godforsaken barbecue, stinking out the whole street to high heaven." She leaned in, and Penny's and Owen's heads instinctively followed her lead. "I'm sure I don't need to remind you that this is a respectable neighbourhood." Her good eye darted between them both.

At that moment, Amy appeared from inside the house, shrieking loudly as Frankie—dressed only in swimming shorts and a Union Jack flag—dropped ice-cubes down the back of her swimsuit.

"Oh, hello, Elsie." Amy came to an abrupt stop, causing Frankie to bump into her and fall flat on his back. In his merry state, he rolled around on the grass, giggling as he blew the cantankerous neighbour a kiss.

"Elsie! Sweetheart! Have you come to join us in the tub?"

Elsie's lips became so tightly pursed they almost disappeared. "As I was saying, this is a *respectable* neighbourhood. Well, it certainly *used* to be." She surveyed the assembled group over the top of her glasses before turning on the heel of her sensible shoe and striding off towards the front door. "Please don't give me any reason to come back here again, or to call the police, which I will not hesitate to do if you create a disturbance."

"Can you believe that woman?" Penny fumed after she'd seen Elsie out. "What a nerve. Honestly!"

"Who's that little ray of sunshine?" asked Nathan.

"Elsie Rayner—she lives two doors down. God, she's dismal." Penny poked at the coals with a little more vehemence than intended and they spat back at her. "You should have seen her when we had the hot tub installed.

She was round here every five minutes, checking we weren't turning the place into a house of ill-repute." She giggled at the memory.

"Oh, don't worry about her." Owen began to place the meat on the barbecue rack and the coals hissed and smoked as meat juices fell onto them. "She's always been the same. Let's just forget about her, okay?"

Penny nodded. "You're right. This is Frankie's day.

On hearing his name, Frankie jumped up from the grass. "Yes, you're right! This is *my* day! *Onward!*"

As he made a dash for the hot tub, Amy pulled him back by the waistband of his shorts, squealing as she overtook him. "Oh, no you don't!"

"Told you she always has to be the first one in, didn't I?" Penny turned to Charlotte. "It's the same every year—she won't give up without a fight."

And that's when—as Charlotte would recall when asked later—everything went into slow motion and became blurred and muddled.

Screams, laughter, the swing coming to a standstill and a splash as Frankie, having overtaken Amy and just a few yards ahead of her, stepped into the hot tub and began to shake.

It took a few seconds for anyone to realise what was happening.

"*Amy!* Don't touch him! Move away!" Nathan called out just in time to stop Amy from pulling Frankie's hand from the metal rail at the side of the tub. "Someone turn off the power, *quickly!*"

Hamburgers, Homicide and a Honeymoon

Pulling Frankie out of the tub, Nathan turned him onto his back and started CPR. "Call an ambulance and get me a blanket or something to keep him warm."

As Penny took a wailing Amy inside, and Danny and Susan kept Zac well away from the drama, the rest of the guests stood in a huddle, the shocked silence broken only by the whimpers coming from Ruby and Eddie.

Sirens signalled the arrival of the emergency services who took over from Nathan.

"What's the name of the gentleman?

Charlotte saw Nathan's shoulders slump as he gave the paramedic a brief shake of his head.

"Frankie. His name's Frankie."

Another siren followed by a brief ring on the doorbell announced the arrival of the police.

"Good afternoon, Sir. We're here in response to a call we've had following a disturbance. Is the ambulance outside also attending the same disturbance?"

"What? Oh, yes…sorry, we've had a terrible shock." As Owen stood back and let the police officers pass, he noticed Elsie hovering outside on the pavement.

By the time the police reached the scene of the accident, the paramedics had stopped CPR.

There was no need for it anymore.

Frankie Ingram was dead

Chapter 3

"I'm Detective Inspector Toby Carter and this is Detective Sergeant Ken Rafferty. Our condolences on the loss of your friend."

Despite the warmth of the day, DI Carter wore a long beige mac, and perspiration beaded his hairline.

"Why are *you* here?" Aidan Pitt puffed out his chest. "This is obviously an accidental death."

"We were called to investigate a disturbance, Sir. Complaints of excessive noise. We had no idea that a death had occurred until we arrived. By all accounts, it seems to be a tragic accident but we'll need to take the names and addresses of everyone here along with a brief witness statement, if they feel up to it." DI Carter glanced into the living room, where an increasingly distraught Amy Baker was refusing any help from the paramedics.

"For goodness' sake, is this absolutely necessary? Surely you can see what happened?" Aidan gestured to Frankie's body under a hastily produced blanket.

"Yes, it is, Sir, but we'll be as quick as we can." DI Carter caught DS Rafferty's eye and spoke under his breath. "Seems like a certain person wants us out of the way, wouldn't you say?"

"I would, Guv," said the Detective Sergeant. "Wonder why that is? One to watch, I'd say."

Charlotte hoped the police would finish whatever it was they needed to do so that she and Nathan could be on their way. She couldn't believe Frankie was dead—it was surreal. One minute he was laughing and joking around and the next, he was gone.

"Nathan," she whispered, tugging at his sleeve. "Is there anything you can do to get us out of here? I feel like we're intruding."

"Yeah, I know what you mean. Just a minute." Nathan approached DI Carter, arm outstretched. "Detective Inspector, my name is Nathan Costello. I'm a guest here, but I'm a DCI in St. Eves in Cornwall. I appreciate that you have a procedure to follow but I wondered if, under the circumstances, you could deal with my wife and I first so we can leave these people in private. We barely knew the deceased, you see—we only met him yesterday—and we feel that our presence here is a little intrusive."

Toby looked Nathan up and down. "A DCI, you say?" He gripped Nathan's hand firmly. "Always good to meet a fellow officer. Okay, we'll take some details from you then you can be on your way. You're not staying here, then?"

"Oh, no." Charlotte winced as she pushed her hand into the small of her back. "We're staying at The Milestone. We're on honeymoon."

"Oh, I see. Congratulations." DI Carter smiled briefly as he wrote in his notebook.

Ten minutes later, he was finished. "Well, I think we've covered everything—we'll be in touch if we have any further questions. Thanks for your time."

As Nathan chatted with the police officers, Charlotte gathered their belongings. She hugged Ruby and said a quick goodbye to the rest of the guests, blowing Penny a kiss but giving her and her sister a wide berth.

Page 47

As she turned away, she was almost sure she saw a smirk on Aidan Pitt's face as he glanced over at Frankie Ingram's lifeless body.

oooooooo

"You okay?" Nathan added a spoonful of honey to a cup of green tea and handed it to Charlotte as she settled herself into one of the hotel bedroom's squashy armchairs.

"No, not really." A warm bath and a lie-down had done little to ease her tension. She sighed. "You know, I could quite easily have packed our bags and gone straight back to St Eves as soon as we left the party. That was horrific. I don't know how you cope with such horrible crimes on a regular basis.

"One minute everything was fine and the next, Frankie was dead. I just can't get my head around it. And poor Amy and Penny and everyone else—I can't imagine how they must be feeling. I felt really bad about leaving the way we did but I felt equally bad about being there."

"I'm sure everyone understood," said Nathan, holding her hand. "We barely knew Frankie, and we barely know the rest of them—I think it would have been weird to have stayed. No one's going to think badly of us for leaving when we did—it's not as though we're going to see any of them again, anyway."

"Well, I'm not so sure about that. Ruby and Penny were talking about dropping into the café some time, so I'm sure I'll see them again even if you don't. Although with what's happened, I don't suppose they'll be in for some time."

"What *did* actually happen?" Nathan pulled another armchair closer to Charlotte. "I was talking to Aidan so I wasn't paying much attention."

Charlotte rubbed her stomach. "I'm not sure. As soon as I realised what was happening, I looked the other way. All I remember is that Amy and Frankie came running out of the house while the rest of us were chatting, and we were laughing at them because Amy was trying to slow him down so she could get in the pool first. And then… that's when it gets confusing, so I can't really remember what happened." She scratched her nose and frowned. "I'll tell you what, though, there are some pretty weird things I *do* remember."

"Oh yes, what things?"

"Well, before Amy went inside to change, I heard her ask Penny if she could borrow one of her swimsuits. One with a high neck."

"And what's strange about that?"

"Didn't you hear Owen talking about the swimsuit Amy wore last year and how small it was? And Ruby saying that Amy had an amazing figure and liked showing it off? And Penny saying she was an exhibitionist? Well, if she was such an exhibitionist, why would she want a high-necked swimsuit that covered everything up?"

Nathan lifted a shoulder. "When it comes to women's fashion, I'm lost, but perhaps she felt like preserving a little modesty. Who knows?" He flicked a peanut into the air and caught it in his mouth. "What else do you remember?"

"Aidan Pitt. When we were getting ready to leave, I'm sure I saw him smirk. You know, kind of smug. As he looked over to where Frankie was, I mean."

"You sure it was a smirk? He strikes me as the type of guy who doesn't show his emotions, so maybe it was just the effort of trying to keep them under control. I can't imagine he intended to come over as smug—he seemed genuinely upset when I spoke to him afterwards."

Charlotte blew on her tea. "Hmmm, maybe. Either way, I don't think I like him very much. He's not very nice to Ruby—he's very dismissive of her."

"That's quite an assumption to make, seeing as we only met the guy today," said Nathan. "And I think it's a little unfair to base an opinion of their entire marriage on an hour spent with them at a barbecue. He's a bit pompous, but he seemed perfectly pleasant otherwise. Actually, he told me there's something he wants to discuss with me when we get back to St. Eves. Can't imagine what it could be—he was very tight-lipped." He picked up another handful of peanuts and crunched on them.

"Anyway, changing the subject, the DI Carter told me they'll be arranging for someone to drain the hot tub to establish the cause of the accident. As if Penny and Amy aren't upset enough, looks like they might have to deal with the fact that Frankie's death was caused by their faulty equipment."

"Oh no! Poor things—what a nightmare. How they're ever going to be able to live with themselves if that's the case—or even go back to the house again—I don't know." Charlotte slid onto Nathan's chair and cuddled up next to him.

He put his arms around her and rubbed her back. "Look, I know how sensitive you are, and I know you're going to be thinking about this for a long time but, please, please try not to get stressed about it. If you want to go home, we'll go home, I don't care about cutting the honeymoon short. I just want you to be wherever you'll be happiest, and most comfortable."

"No, I think I'm okay," said Charlotte after a pause. "I wanted to go home straight after it happened, but I'm not sure now. Perhaps I'll feel differently tomorrow but, for now, I think I'd like to stay. We're going to have so little time to ourselves soon, so I want to finish our honeymoon." She looked up at Nathan. "As long as you do?"

"If you're happy to stay, then I'm happy to stay. Now, how about we order room service? We can watch a film, or you can read your book, I'll give you a back rub, and we can get some sleep?"

Charlotte nodded. "That sounds good. I don't think I could face going down to the restaurant after what's happened and I really don't feel like going out."

"Perfect," said Nathan. "Room service it is, then!"

ooooooo

After a long discussion, Charlotte and Nathan decided that despite recent events, they would try to enjoy the rest of their honeymoon as much as possible.

Over their room service dinner of seared salmon salad for Nathan, and roast turbot with lemon sauce, pickled onions, mushy peas, and a side order of Spam fritters for Charlotte, they'd concluded that, while Frankie's tragic death had affected them both, neither of them wanted it to put an end to their honeymoon.

The following morning, they set off after a hearty breakfast, determined to make the most of another glorious day. Having walked for miles and feeling decidedly peckish, they were watching a juggling magician in Covent Garden when the smell of fried onions wafted past Charlotte's nose and woke one of her dormant cravings.

Sniffing the air, she followed the smell. "Oh my…do you mind if we find out where that's coming from?"

They tracked the mouth-watering aroma to a small shop, bearing the sign, *Big Al's Diner: Established 1980. Proprietor: Alan King.*

"Well, it must be good if it's been here so long. Wonder if Big Al's around today?" Charlotte peered in through the large shopfront window at the young man in a black apron and hat, flipping large, ground-steak patties on one side of a vast griddle, the other half of which contained a mound of lightly caramelised onions.

"Well, I don't know about you, but I know what I'm having for lunch," she said. "I'm drooling already."

"They look busy but we can wait for a table inside. Come on." Nathan held the door open and they entered a small entrance lobby which opened up into a large space, furnished with chrome fixtures, red leather-look seats, and red and white checked cloths covering the Formica-topped tables.

In complete contrast to the formal waiting staff of the hotel, the servers were dressed in white t-shirts, cut off Levi's, and roller skates.

As they waited to be seated, a cheerful server sped towards them.

"Hi, my name's Billy, I'll be your server…" His smile quickly faded as he realised he might not be able to stop in time to avoid a collision.

Anticipating the possible outcome, Nathan stood in front of Charlotte, his arms outstretched and the server grabbed onto his hands.

"Oh, blimey, I'm so sorry." The young boy's face turned pink. "I only started a few days ago and I haven't quite got the hang of these skates yet. It's okay, though," he assured, quickly. "I'm not allowed to carry any food yet. I'm on greet and seat duty for a couple of weeks till I've finished my training."

He looked over his shoulder before whispering, "You won't tell my granddad, will you? He gave me this job after I finished my exams, you know just to give me some extra cash, but if he finds out I lied to him, he'll be really upset."

Charlotte grinned. "Let me guess, you told him you could roller skate. Am I right?"

The boy scratched the back of his neck and nodded, sheepishly. "I didn't think it would be so hard to learn—but I *am* getting better."

"Hmm, it's not the skating you seem to have a problem with," Nathan observed. "It's the stopping. "But don't worry," he tapped his nose, "we won't say a word."

Looking a little happier, the young boy grabbed two menus from a stand. "Would you like a table? I'm afraid it'll be about twenty minutes, but you can have a drink at the bar and decide what you'd like to eat while you wait."

"Yes, please, we'll do that. After seeing those burgers, I'm not leaving until I've had one!" Charlotte eyed a platter holding ten mini-burgers, a bucket of shoestring fries, and a bubbling dish of macaroni cheese as it zoomed past her on its way to a table.

"Well, I'll get you seated as soon as I can. Till then, you can sit and talk to my granddad—or should I say, he can talk to you," said Billy, treating them to a mischief-filled grin.

Charlotte and Nathan followed him to a gleaming stainless steel-topped bar occupied by other waiting customers, behind which stood a man they presumed was Big Al.

Pale-faced, sandy-haired, and blue-eyed, Big Al wore a red and white checked shirt, a dazzling white apron, a white chef's cap set at a jaunty angle and a smile that stretched from ear-to-ear. Despite being deep in conversation with a customer at the bar, his eyes darted around the diner, keeping an eye on everything.

Charlotte doubted that much went on that Big Al missed… apart from the fact that his grandson couldn't roller skate to save his life.

"Hey! New friends! Come, come and sit down and take the weight off—oh, hold on, lady with a baby comin' through!" He put down the glass he was polishing and rushed around to the other side of the bar. Holding out his hand, he helped Charlotte onto a stool. "You settled? You comfortable? Good. Now, what can I get you? First drink to all new friends is on the house. Courtesy of Big Al." He pointed to himself with his thumbs. "That's me, in case you hadn't guessed."

He chuckled all the way back to behind the bar, where he leaned over and stared at Nathan and Charlotte through narrowed eyes. "Now, don't tell me…" He rubbed his chin. "You," he said, nodding in Nathan's direction. "I reckon you're a light beer man. Am I right or am I right?"

Nathan nodded. "Very impressive. I am."

Big Al looked pleased with himself. "And the lady, I reckon she'd like a cocktail—non-alcoholic of course. Somethin' a little fruity with a splash of coconut perhaps?"

"Sounds delicious." Charlotte smiled. "You've got me well figured out."

"Yeah, well, it's my business to know what my customers want," said Al, smiling widely as he filled a fish bowl glass with peach pulp, cubed pineapple, and raspberries, and topped it up with coconut water, ginger ale, a splash of strawberry syrup, and a drizzle of grenadine. He decorated it with a cocktail stirrer, a paper umbrella and a lit sparkler, and slid it across the bar.

"So, you here on holiday? I know you don't live 'round here 'cos if you did, you'd have been in before."

"It's our first time in London," said Charlotte. "We're on our honeymoon." Aware that she was rubbing her baby bump, she followed with, "We got married in December but we've only just got round to getting away."

Big Al put his hands up. "Hey, I'm not judging! Love is a wonderful thing, whenever it happens and whatever order it happens in. So, where you staying?

"The Milestone… and this cocktail is gorgeous!" Charlotte speared a pineapple cube with the end of her stirrer.

"Nice. I worked in their kitchen years ago," said Al. "First-class in every respect but I'm not sure they were ready for a youngster like me and his off-the-wall ideas when it came to creatin' new dishes for the menu. You know what I mean?" He winked and picked up another glass to dry. "So, you been seein' the sights since you've been here?"

Charlotte nodded. "Yep, and we've got a lot more to see. We're tourists while we're here so going to cram in as much as we can before we go home."

"Well, if you wanna know anything about anything, you come and ask me 'cos there ain't much that goes on around here that I don't know about. Same goes for the people—I pretty much know 'em all."

"Thanks, that's good of you," said Nathan, "but we're not going to be here for long enough to get to know anyone, so I don't think we're going to be needing any character references. But thanks all the same."

Al tipped his cap. "Don't mention it. Always happy to point people in the right direction if I can."

A broad-shouldered delivery man pushing a barrow loaded with boxes of chuck steak distracted Al on his way through to the kitchen.

"Hey, Al," he said, in an accent even broader than the proprietor's. "You hear that Frankie Ingram got fried in Penny Baker's hot tub yesterday? It's all over the TV. Talk about some people bein' a magnet for bad luck." He pulled a large handkerchief from his back pocket and wiped his forehead.

Al spread his arms wide. "Jimmy, I got customers here." He gestured towards Charlotte and Nathan. "These people are on their honeymoon. They don't wanna hear about some poor guy who croaked his last in a hot tub—you know what I mean?" He put his hands on his ample hips and shook his head as the delivery man disappeared into the kitchen with a sheepish expression on his face.

"Sorry about that," said Al. "Some people don't know when to give their big mouths a rest."

"It's okay. Don't worry about it." Charlotte poked around in her glass for more fruit. "Actually, we already know about it—we were at Penny's when it happened."

Immediately, Al's smile vanished. "You're friends of Penny Baker?"

His reaction took Charlotte by surprise. "No, not friends, just acquaintances—we met at the airport on the way out here—but we got chatting and, when we bumped into her a couple of days ago, she invited us to her house for a barbecue. We barely know her, really."

"And you was at the barbecue? When poor Frankie… oh jeez!" Al slapped his sausage-like fingers against his forehead and sat down heavily on a stool behind the bar.

"Unfortunately, we were," said Nathan. "So you know Penny and Frankie?"

"Yeah, and Amy, too." Al nodded. "The girls don't come in here no more, though—it's a long story—but whenever Frankie came back to London, he always dropped by to chew the fat and to grab a couple'a burgers. In fact, only a few days ago, he was sittin' right where you're sittin' now."

"What d'you mean, when he "came back" to London?" asked Charlotte.

"He used to live 'round here, years ago," said Al. "So did Penny and Amy. Frankie left first and the girls followed soon afterwards." He inspected his fingernails.

"Can't say I was sorry to see the back of them, either. Penny and Amy, I mean. Devious pair, if ever I met one."

He crooked his index finger, drawing them closer. "Mr and Mrs Baker—the parents—now, they're lovely people. She's an interior designer and he's got his own private investigation company. Years ago, he was workin' on an investigation—the client had hired him to follow her husband 'cos she was sure he was havin' an affair, and…" He scratched his head. "Well, turns out he *was* havin' an affair. He was havin' an affair with Penny."

He shook his head again. "Oh boy, it caused a lot of trouble at the time. Thing is, she used to come in here with the guy all the time—they'd sit canoodlin' in a booth, makin' a burger and a rootbeer last all evenin'. She was single, seventeen but looked twenty-five—and turned out he was married, thirty-three but looked twenty. How was I s'posed to know he was so much older than her? He looked young enough to me and he didn't wear no wedding ring. Anyway, her dad was mortified—I don't know how he explained *that* to his client—and Penny was grounded for months.

"Anyone else would have learned their lesson after that, but not Penny. Oh, no." Big Al's big jowls wobbled as he shook his head. "She only started carryin' on with the guy again and, when she finished with him, she took up with another older guy. Her parents was at their wits' end, worryin' about her and the bad influence she was havin' on her sister, Amy. The last thing they wanted was for Amy to follow Penny's lead and find an old 'friend' of her own—you know what I mean?

"Anyway, me and my Lynne, that's my wife, we told the Bakers we'd give the girls a few hours workin' here in the evenin' if it would help put their minds at rest. They were goin' crazy worryin' about where they were, what they were doin', and who they were doin' it with—if you know what I mean. We told 'em we'd keep an eye on the girls here. That way, they could be sure they weren't gettin' up to no mischief."

"Why'd you give Penny a job if she was so much trouble?" asked Nathan.

Al shrugged. "'Cos I felt kinda responsible, I s'pose. Knowin' she'd been carryin' on with the guy under my nose made me feel a little stupid, you know? I guess I gave her a job by way of an apology to Mr and Mrs Baker—my Lynne told me to keep out of it but I felt like I had to do somethin'."

"So why'd you pull a face when I mentioned her name?" said Charlotte, twirling a cocktail umbrella.

Al picked up another glass from the draining tray. "Well, she and Amy had been workin' here a few months when we noticed the tips were lower than usual. Our servers have always made great tips, so the drop was really noticeable."

"Don't tell me—Penny had her hand in the tip jar?" said Nathan.

Al nodded. "You got it in one—and Amy, too. They shoulda been puttin' the tips in the jar behind the bar to get shared out between all the servers at the end of the night, but they was puttin' 'em in their own pockets instead.

"When I found out what was goin' on, I felt like I'd been kicked in the teeth. I trusted 'em and they threw it back in my face. The day I found out was the last day they worked here. We lost customers, too—a lot of their friends used to come here to eat when they was workin' but, after I booted the girls out, they stopped comin'. Mind you, I'm not sure that was a bad thing—my Lynne was convinced that half of 'em were eating for nothin', if you know what I mean."

For a fleeting moment he looked troubled, but his frown was soon replaced by a smile. "Anyways, not my place to tell you who to hang around with and who not to, just giving you the benefit of my experience. You seem like nice people, so I wouldn't want you gettin' stung like we did. Sometimes you just gotta look at the bigger picture to see what's going on right under your nose, you know what I mean?"

He looked over Charlotte's shoulder at his grandson, who was rolling towards them at a frightening speed.

"Hey, looks like your table might be ready. You enjoy your meal. Oh, and don't forget to read about the competition on the back of your menu in case you're interested in takin' part."

"What competition?" asked Charlotte.

"If you can guess the secret ingredient in the burgers, you'll get one meal on the house." Al chuckled. "But if you think you know, don't go shoutin' out the answer—just tell a server and they'll let you know if you're right. The competition's been runnin' for over thirty years, and in all that time only fourteen people have guessed what it is.

"And by the way, if you're thinkin' of havin' a side order with your main, we do a great macaroni cheese with bacon—it's my own recipe and it's to die for, if I do say so myself. Anyway, nice talkin' to you."

"Likewise." Nathan helped Charlotte down from the stool. "If these burgers are as good as they look, I'm sure we'll see you again before we go home."

"If they're as good as they look, we'll *definitely* see you again—and I'm definitely up for the culinary challenge." Charlotte licked her lips as a waitress rolled past them with a platter bearing a juicy burger complete with melted cheese, sliced pickles, crispy homemade fries, a house salad, handmade relish and coleslaw and, the crowning glory as far as Charlotte was concerned, a pile of glossy, deep-golden fried onions. She jabbed the air with a determined finger. "*That's* what I'm having. Come on—let's eat!"

ooooooo

"Those burgers were, without a doubt, the best I've ever tasted. They're going on the menu when we get home." Charlotte fanned her face.

"I can't believe you guessed what the ingredient was," said Nathan as he hung off the strap on the crowded underground train. "I knew there was something different about them but I would never have guessed what. In fact, if I'd known beforehand, I'm not sure I'd have tried them."

"I think it's because my senses have heightened since I've been pregnant—well, my sense of taste and smell, at least. I'm not sure I'd have known otherwise. Anyway, Al's a character, isn't he? Surprising what he said about Penny and Amy, don't you think? Mind you, I'm not judging—we all made mistakes when we were kids."

"Well, it's not really surprising because we don't know them, do we?" said Nathan. "Maybe they still do stuff like that now—how would we know? That's the thing when you don't have a history with someone—you have to take them at face value and hope they're being honest with you. If they're convincing enough, they can make you believe that the most far-fetched lies are the truth. How would you ever know any different? Anyway, come on, here's our stop."

oooooooo

Later that evening, after a twilight circuit on the London Eye followed by a light dinner and a hot chocolate in a restaurant overlooking the River Thames, Charlotte fell into an uneasy sleep.

Her dreams were filled with images of corpses and electric chairs.

A figure in black, menacingly brandishing a triple-decker burger, removed a hood to reveal the sombre face of Big Al. 'Sometimes you just gotta look at the bigger picture to see what's going on right under your nose,' he reminded her.

Twice, she woke in a hot sweat, thoughts of recent events spinning around in her head. A nagging feeling of unease started to settle in and she suddenly craved to be surrounded by all things familiar—to be back in St. Eves in her own home with Jess, Ava, Betty, and Harriet to make her laugh.

On the verge of waking Nathan, she decided against it. Instead, she pulled the duvet up to her chin and, just as dawn's misty veil fell away to reveal the day, she dozed off into a troubled sleep.

oooooooo

"I feel a little ungrateful saying it, but I'm so glad we're leaving today." Charlotte winced as the baby gave her a kick any football fan would have been proud of. "I'm ready to go home now."

"Well, wait no more, my love." Nathan opened the taxi door and helped her into the backseat. "St. Eves, here we come."

With every mile closer to the airport they got, Charlotte felt her heart become a little lighter, her mood remaining upbeat until she saw Penny in the departure lounge, on her own and looking lost, holding Zac in a baby sling.

"Listen, if going over there to say hello is going to upset you, don't go," said Nathan. "She'll never know—damn it, she's seen us."

Penny waved before making a beeline for them.

"Hi, how are you?" Charlotte tickled Zac's arm as he leaned his head against Penny's shoulder, eyelids drooping over big blue eyes as he sucked on his thumb.

"Oh, you know. In a daze, really. We still can't believe what's happened. We're just going through the motions. You know, I thought the police were going to arrest us—or at least keep us here. I was so relieved when they said we could go home—I know we're going to be hearing from them again soon, though." She blinked back the tears that were threatening to fall and lifted her chin towards her sister. "It's Amy I'm worried about. She's taken it so hard. She feels completely to blame."

"What? Why on earth would she feel that?" said Charlotte.

"Because she thinks Frankie's dead because he overtook her and got in the tub first. If she hadn't let him catch her up, he'd still be here."

"Yes, but she'd be the one lying on a mortuary slab. For goodness' sake, she can't think like that—she'll drive herself mad."

"I know, Charlotte. We've all told her that but..." Penny shook her head and stroked Zac's hair. "Anyway, I just wanted to come and say hello. I'm so sorry you had to be a part of all this—I hope it didn't ruin your honeymoon, although I suspect it probably did."

"Look, don't worry about it." Charlotte hugged her. "If you ever want a change of scene back in St. Eves, you'll find me at *Charlotte's Plaice* café on the marina every day except Saturday."

Penny managed a smile. "Okay, thanks—that'd be nice. Zac will love the boats and I might even drag Amy and Ruby along, too." She squeezed Charlotte's hand. "See you back in St. Eves."

CHAPTER 4

"I can't tell you how happy I am to be back!" Charlotte pounced on Jess and hugged her till she squeaked, before bursting into tears.

"Ouch, you're squeezing the air out of me!" Jess grinned as she rubbed her ribs. "Hey, what's wrong?" She passed Charlotte a serviette from the bar and gave her a hug.

"Oh, don't take any notice of me—it's just hormones and being glad to see you!"

"Well, as long as that's all it is. So, did you have a good time?"

"Yes…and no. Oh, my gosh, I don't know where to start." Charlotte dried her eyes. "Let's get set up and I'll fill you in on everything. You won't believe what happened!"

With Pippin at her feet and a mug of tea in her hand, Charlotte sat on the terrace and told Jess everything about the eventful visit to London.

"Oh, my God! So he was electrocuted? And he was the tattoo artist from that place just outside town?"

Charlotte nodded as she sipped her tea. "Honestly, Jess, it was awful. He seemed like such a nice guy."

"Did he have a wife or a girlfriend?"

"Well, he was very friendly with one of the girls who was there. I'm not sure, but I think they might have been in a relationship. She was terribly upset, that's for sure." Charlotte checked the time on her phone. "Well, I suppose we'd better get ready to open—looks like it's going to be another beautiful day and you know what the sun brings…"

"Punters!" said Jess, pushing open the sliding glass doors that separated the outside terrace from the inside café, creating a long, seamless space.

As Charlotte looked out at the view of the boats in the marina, resplendent in the sunshine, she knew it would be a long time before she'd want to leave St. Eves for any length of time again. She loved her friends and her little café and she'd missed them both while she'd been away.

"Ooh, I forgot to tell you, I'm adding something to the menu. We had the most amazing burgers in London in an old diner and they had an ingredient you wouldn't usually associate with burgers, but it gave them the most incredible flavour. I'm calling them Big Al's Burgers, after the owner—he said I could use his name. Anyway, I'll make one for you later and you can tell me if you can guess what the secret ingredient is."

As she settled Pippin's basket in its usual place, just outside the café at the top of the terrace, she was pounced on by Ava Whittington, long-time resident, loyal customer and good friend.

"Charlotte, my dear, you're back! Oh, we've missed you—it just wasn't the same without you here."

Charlotte giggled as she noted the sideways look Jess gave the old woman.

"Erm, not that Jess and Laura didn't do a *marvellous* job in your absence—of course they did—but it's nice that everything's back to normal. Now, let me look at you." She held Charlotte at arm's length. "You're looking a little peaky, dear. Are you feeling alright?" Without waiting for an answer, she carried on talking.

"Anyway, I wanted to ask about your baby shower. It's still all set for next Saturday, isn't it?"

"Yes. Why?"

"Because I want to bake a cake to bring along with me. Right, I've got an appointment to have my ears syringed so I must fly or I'll be late. Toodle-pip, my dears, I'll see you later. Or should I say, I'll *hear* you later? Ha! Ta-ta for now."

Jess looked on as the elderly woman tip-tapped away on elegant court shoes. "Has there been a hurricane 'Ava' yet? Because if there hasn't, there flippin' well should be!"

ooooooo

"Talk about an eventful start to married life!"

Charlotte's Plaice regulars, Leo Reeves and Harry Jenkins leaned against the bar.

"I thought a honeymoon was about getting away from it all!" said Harry.

"Well, I can assure you," said Charlotte as she put down two bowls of French onion soup with homemade crusty bread in front of two of her favourite customers, "this one wasn't! We had a fabulous time but that sort of took the edge off it, as you can imagine."

"Hmmm, I *can* imagine." Leo dunked a large piece of bread into his soup and scooped up a pile of onions and melted cheese.

"So, you say these people live locally?" said Harry. "The people you met there, I mean. Any of them ever come in here? Anyone Leo and I might have chatted to?"

Charlotte nodded. "Well, Eddie's been in once before with his mum but I don't think you'll know him. I don't think you'll know any of them apart from one, maybe—Aidan Pitt. You know who I mean, don't you? He moved to St. Eves a few years ago. He used to be a co-presenter on some money programme but don't ask me which one because I can't remember."

"You're joking? Aidan Pitt?" Leo reached for a serviette. "Good God, don't tell Ava and Harriett, for goodness' sake. You'll start a riot."

"Why?"

"Because they're *huge* Aidan Pitt fans."

"Really?" Charlotte exchanged a surprised look with Jess. "I've never heard them talk about him."

"Well, between you and me," said Leo, "they're not *quite* as keen as those women they hang around with sometimes, but you know Ava—the first whiff of a celebrity and she's bought the t-shirt. You know the women I mean, don't you? That group who keep track of Aidan Pitt's every move, and spend every waking minute gossiping about him since he moved to St. Eves. What are they called, now? 'The Pittettes' or something equally ridiculous." He finished his mouthful before continuing.

"I happened to be round at Harriett's one afternoon when a few of them dropped in and they were such a strange bunch of women, I made myself scarce. Like robots, they were, all programmed with encyclopaedic data about Aidan Pitt that they could recall at the drop of a hat. They were very creepy, I can tell you—I couldn't wait to get out of there."

"I don't know about creepy—I'd call it weird," said Jess. "I mean, what good will knowing everything there is to know about Aidan Pitt ever do anyone?"

oooooo

The hectic breakfast service was almost at an end when a familiar voice called through to the kitchen.

"Hi, Charlotte. We're not staying long, we just dropped by to say hello."

She raised her head to see Penny and Amy in the café, Zac slung around Penny's neck in his sling.

"Oh, hi! You made it! Um, why don't you go and grab a table somewhere and I'll be out to see you in minute? Jess, this is Penny, Amy, and Zac—some of the people we met while we were away."

"Oh, hi. Nice to meet you." Jess fussed over Zac, took the drinks orders, and suggested that Charlotte take the weight off her feet while there were no more food orders to cook.

"Okay, I will take a break, but give me a shout if you need me for anything." As she pulled up a chair at the sisters' table, she saw how drawn they looked. Amy, in particular, had dark circles in the deep hollows under her eyes, and her skin was pale and pasty-looking. She looked so lost, Charlotte couldn't help but lean across and give her a hug.

"How are you?"

Amy shook her head. "Not great. And what's even worse is that I don't think it will really hit me until the funeral." Her eyes welled up and she waved her hand in front of her face. "Sorry, I can't stop bursting into tears. If I could just stop thinking about it..."

"Goodness, there's no need to apologise," said Charlotte.

Amy gave her a grateful smile and blew her nose. "Can we change the subject, please? It's all everyone's talked about since it happened and I'm not in a very good place right now." She leaned sideways to look inside the bar. "Is that the ladies room, that door on the left? I won't be long."

Penny waited until her sister was out of earshot. "Sorry to turn up when neither of us is at our best. I thought a change of scene would do us both good, but it was such an effort to get Amy here, I almost didn't think we'd make it. Since it happened, she hasn't wanted to go anywhere or do anything. She just wants to lie in bed. I had to literally drag her out of it to come down here with Zac and me.

"I know Frankie's only been gone for a week, but I know what she's like—she'll sit and think about what happened and analyse it for hours—particularly as she thinks it was her fault anyway. She'll end up making herself ill if she's not careful, I know she will." Penny blinked quickly and held onto Zac's hands as she lifted him up and down on her feet.

"Well, I can understand why she's so upset," said Charlotte, "losing her partner in such terrible circumstances."

Penny shook her head. "Oh, no, Frankie wasn't her partner—not even a casual boyfriend." She half-smiled and lifted Zac onto her lap. "You're not the only one to think there was something between them, but they were just friends. Very close but just friends. They've known each other since they were kids—they adored each other.

"He was the reason we came here from London, really. He came because he wanted to be somewhere that inspired his creativity and Amy missed him so much that, a year later, we joined him. It was easy for her to get bar work down here, and I'm a freelance writer so I can work wherever I want to. When Amy said she was moving down, I had nothing to lose by packing up and coming with her. And then I met Owen here and the rest is history. Anyway, it did us good to get away from London—it's so peaceful. I find that I'm a lot more productive here and since Owen gave up his job to be a house-husband, which he absolutely loves, the lifestyle suits us both down to the ground."

Amy re-joined them and Penny stood Zac up on her lap. "Look, it's Aunty Amy!" The little boy gurgled happily and held out his arms, eliciting a sad smile from the young woman.

"Come on, let's go and have a look at the boats, shall we?" said Amy, lifting the little boy into a hug.

"Just a minute." Charlotte went inside, reappearing a minute later with a small bag of bread. "Here. You'll need this to feed the fish. You'll see them in the water all along the marina-front."

"Thank you. That's sweet of you." Amy gave the bag of bread to Zac, who promptly put a piece in his mouth. "If there's any left for the fish, I'm sure they'll enjoy it."

"So, is your house in London all locked up now or do the police still need access to it?" Charlotte asked Penny as they watched Zac empty the whole bag of bread into the water at once.

"Yes, it's locked up, but Owen's cousin, Danny, has a key so we've left him in charge. Thank God for him and Susan—there was no way we could stay at the house after what happened, so we all went to stay at their place until it was time to come home.

"The police were going to arrange for the hot tub to be drained so someone could make it safe, and to find out what the cause of the accident was. It's only four years old but, between you and me, I've got a bad feeling about it." Penny blinked hard and focused on Zac. "Anyway, we'll just have to wait and see what they find out—what will be will be, I guess."

Charlotte noticed Penny's mood visibly lighten as Zac toddled towards her.

"Well, that didn't last long." Amy shook a few crumbs from the bread bag, the beginning of a smile curving her lips.

Penny checked her watch. "Do me a favour, will you? Put Zac in his pushchair while I go to the ladies room. And then we'd better be going. I won't be a minute."

As Charlotte watched Amy quickly secure Zac into the seat with straps and buckles, she wondered how long it would take her to become as adept.

"You know, it's so beautiful here, I don't know why we don't come more often," said Amy, a smile spreading across her face for the first time that afternoon. "We'll definitely visit again, but we'll bring our own bread next time, won't we, Zac?" She leaned forward for a baby wipe from the bag underneath the seat and Zac clutched hold of her t-shirt in a tight little fist. As she curled open his fingers, he pulled the front of the shirt down and Charlotte caught sight of a tattoo on Amy's chest.

Still pink around the edges, it looked fairly new. It was a heart enclosing the initials AB & FI.

Amy Baker and Frankie Ingram. Why would Amy have a tattoo of Frankie's initials if there'd been nothing between them? Very strange.

"Right, we must be off." Penny interrupted her musings. "We're going to take Zac for a long walk along the beach. Nice to see you again, Charlotte."

"Likewise. Look, I'm having a baby shower next Saturday—if you'd like to come, you're very welcome. It's at *Fisherman's Cottage* on the seafront. You know *The President* hotel? Well, it's just past there, on the opposite side of the road. Around one o'clock, if you're interested—it should be good fun. And bring Zac along if you come—there'll be plenty of people there who'll be only too happy to take him off your hands for a couple of hours." She smiled as she thought of Ava, Harriett, Betty, and Laura cooing over the little boy.

"Okay, thanks, maybe we will—it'll be something to look forward to, won't it, Amy? Right, say bye-bye to Charlotte, Zac."

As Charlotte waved the girls off, she couldn't stop thinking about Amy's tattoo.

"They seem like nice people," said Jess, passing a cup of tea to Charlotte as she came back into the café. "You can see how upset the younger one is, can't you? I assume she's the girl you were talking about earlier? The one who was seeing the tattooist?"

"Hmmm." Charlotte nodded. "Yes, she's the one I was talking about, but turns out she wasn't seeing him after all. Well, not according to her sister, anyway. Question for you. You're friends with Nathan, aren't you? You've known him for years."

"Yes, of course I am. Why?"

Page 73

"Would it ever occur to you to get a tattoo with his initials in it? Or of anyone you were really good friends with? Or fond of? In a big heart? Sort of here?" She touched her fingers to the top of her bra.

The look on Jess's face answered the question.

"A tattoo of Nathan's initials in a big heart? Erm, funnily enough, no, the thought's never occurred to me. I wouldn't even get a tattoo of mine and Ben's initials."

"I thought not. It'd be too weird, wouldn't it?" Charlotte frowned as she chopped salad vegetables.

I must remember to tell Nathan about it later.

oooooooo

"So, how was your first day back at work? I hope you didn't overdo it?" Nathan kissed Charlotte before making a fuss of Pippin.

"It was bliss. It was so nice to see everyone. I know we were only away for two weeks but it felt like so much longer after the accident. What about you? Good day?"

"Yeah, not bad. A lot of catching up on casework, but okay."

"And you'll never guess."

Nathan looked up from Pippin, who was lying spread-eagled on the floor, enjoying having his tummy tickled. "Charlotte, I hate it when you say that. No, you're right, I'll never guess."

She grinned. "Penny and Amy came in today with Zac."

"Really? I *am* surprised. I didn't think you'd see them again."

"Well, they said they'd drop in but I wasn't entirely convinced they would."

"Are they okay?"

Charlotte pulled a face. "Well, Penny seems okay but she's worried about Amy. She's not doing at all well—very down in the dumps. Understandably, of course. I'll tell you something odd, though. You know we thought Amy and Frankie were an item? Well, Penny said they weren't—they've just been really close friends for years."

"Oh. Well, I wouldn't say it was odd, but it's surprising," said Nathan. "Considering how tactile they were with each other."

"No, *that* isn't what's odd. What's odd is that Amy's got Frankie's initials in a tattoo on her chest. I saw it when Zac pulled the neck of her t-shirt down. I'm no expert but it looks like she only had it done fairly recently. Anyway, if there was nothing between them, why the tattoo?"

Nathan shrugged. "No idea. Maybe she had a thing for him that she hadn't told anyone about? Or maybe they were in a *secret* relationship which is why her sister didn't know about it? Or maybe it was just because they were such close friends? Friends often have tattoos of each other's names these days, don't they?"

He frowned. "Actually, speaking of tattoos, apart from all the others he had, Frankie also had one on his finger that I thought was unusual. This finger." He waggled his wedding ring at Charlotte. "I noticed it when I was trying to resuscitate him."

"Oh? What did it say?"

"Together."

"Together? Together, what?" said Charlotte. "What's that supposed to mean? You sure it didn't say anything else?"

"Yes, I'm sure. That's why I thought it was unfinished." Nathan checked the time, stood up and stretched. "I'm going to get changed and get in a quick run before dinner. Won't be long."

Five minutes later he was clamping his headphones over his ears. "I'll be back in a bit. Oh, and can you call your aunt? She accidentally rang my number instead of yours this afternoon. She wants to talk to you about the baby shower and she asked when she could come and stay for a while after the baby's born."

"Oh, that's great—I'll call her while you're out." Charlotte's face lit up. Since Nathan had tracked down her long-lost Aunt Lola before their wedding, they'd kept in regular contact and Charlotte was thrilled that she and her two cousins had become permanent fixtures in her life since then.

As the front door slammed, all thoughts of Penny, Amy, Frankie, and mysterious tattoos disappeared as she dialled her aunt's number.

CHAPTER 5

Ever since amassing his considerable fortune, Aidan Pitt had been paranoid that someone would try to take it away from him, break into his home, or try to kidnap him.

His state-of-the-art security systems were the best money could buy and, over the years, he had taken every precaution to keep himself, his antiques, his priceless art collection, and his money well protected.

Since moving to St. Eves, he had felt safe—much safer than when he'd lived in big cities. All his adult life, he'd been careful to surround himself with staff he could trust implicitly but, in Eddie, he was sure he'd found the ultimate employee—loyal, trustworthy, and discreet, but intimidating enough to deter anyone who might be thinking of getting a little too up close and personal with him.

He knew he could trust Eddie with his life, and with any confidence, but the secret around which his current dilemma revolved was too secret to divulge to even Eddie.

He had to find out who knew what had happened all those years ago, and deal with it on his own.

As he thought about it, the veins on his forehead bulged. That someone thought they could get one over on him made him furious.

And vulnerable.

He logged into his email account to read the message again.

I know what you did.
I know what you did all those years ago.

You have until the end of June to make amends with those you hurt so deeply.

If you fail to do so, I will go to the press with my story and you can kiss your reputation goodbye.

Remember—the end of June. Not a day later.

He closed the lid on his laptop and rested his chin on clasped fingers. He didn't want to involve the police, but he wanted their protection. Only on his terms, though.

He picked up his phone and dialled the number Nathan had given him when they'd spoken in London.

"DCI Costello, please. It's Aidan Pitt. What? Yes, I'll hold. Good morning, Detective Chief Inspector. Very well, thank you. You recall I mentioned that I wanted to see you? Well I'd like to arrange a meeting as soon as possible—at the station, preferably. I'd rather Ruby didn't know I was meeting with you. Right, half-past three this afternoon. Okay, I'll see you then."

oooooo

"What is it I can do for you?" Nathan sat across the desk from Aidan Pitt.

"I'll get straight to the point. You must know that I'm a very wealthy, very successful man. And you must know that one doesn't make the sort of money I have without making a few enemies along the way. It's inevitable that many people who have not been as fortunate as me will envy what I have. Some will wish me bad fortune. And some will try to take what I have and tarnish my reputation."

He paused to gauge Nathan's reaction but his expression was impassive.

"The thing is… I believe that someone is out to do just that—which is the reason for my visit. I believe that someone wishes me harm and I want you to guarantee my safety."

Nathan frowned. "So, you've had threats made against you? Verbal or physical?"

Aidan shook his head. "No. No threats, it's just a feeling I have—my intuition tells me that all is not well."

He had no intention of telling Nathan about the email threatening to expose his secret. He just wanted the police to maintain a presence and for the blackmailer to be aware of it. He had no idea of their location, of course, but he hoped that if they were keeping as close tabs on him as he imagined they were, the involvement of the police would scare them off. After all, the penalty for blackmail was harsh.

"I understand how this must seem, Detective Chief Inspector. I come to you with this crazy notion that my life or, at the very least, my reputation, is under threat. Unfortunately, I have no evidence that this is the case, nor can I supply you with the names of any potential guilty parties. All I can tell you is that I have a profound sense of doom that, try as I might, I cannot shake off."

He crossed his legs and picked an unruly piece of lint from the knee of his impeccably pressed trousers. "So, what can you do to vouch for my safety? I was thinking of a couple of officers stationed permanently outside the house, but I'll defer to your better judgement. I haven't yet told Ruby of my concerns—I'll wait until the officers arrive—but I know she'll feel much more relaxed about the situation just knowing there are policeman standing guard."

Nathan's face took on a bemused expression as he scratched his chin. "You'll forgive me if I recap briefly, won't you? I just want to make sure I understand exactly what it is you're asking for." He drummed the pads of his fingers together.

"You want me to extend the personal services of two police officers to you because you have a completely unfounded, yet "profound sense of doom" that someone is out to cause you harm? Is that correct?"

Aidan nodded. "That's about the measure of it, yes. So, what can you do?"

Nathan shook his head. "I can do nothing, I'm afraid, Mr Pitt. I'm not about to stretch our already limited resources based on your whim. If you could give me something with which to back up your concerns, I'd be happy to discuss the matter with you, but, with nothing more to go on than your intuition, all I'm prepared to do is ask a car to patrol the area more often. If you could give me even the slightest proof that you, or your wife, are in any danger, then, of course, we'd have something to discuss."

Aidan wasn't accustomed to not getting his own way. He wasn't used to people refusing to accommodate him. Usually, he had only to ask and his wish was granted. He wasn't happy. Not at all.

"I see." His voice was frosty. "So, you are refusing to help a resident in need of police protection?"

Nathan sighed.

"Mr Pitt. If you were in danger, or the victim of a campaign of harassment, I can assure that my best officers would already be on the case. But, as neither applies, there is little I can do except to ask a patrol car to drive past your home on a more regular basis."

Aidan stood up, his body language a clear expression of his discontent. "Right." "Well I won't waste any more of my time." His tone was clipped. "Good afternoon to you."

As Nathan's assistant, Amanda, accompanied him from the building, a mild feeling of panic bubbled in his gut.

He still had no idea as to the identity of his mysterious blackmailer and, without a police presence to act as a deterrent to the extortionist, there was every chance that his dark secret would be exposed at the end of the month.

ooooooo

Four days after his return to the station, Amanda put a late afternoon call through to Nathan's office from DI Toby Carter.

"Good afternoon, Nathan. How's sunny St. Eves?" The Detective Inspector's gruff south London accent boomed down the line.

Nathan chuckled. "We get our fair share of sunshine, but something tells me you're not calling to talk about the weather."

"I wish I was," said Toby. "No, it's a courtesy call to let you know that Ken and I will be coming down tomorrow morning to collect some DNA samples."

"Oh yes. Why's that, then?" asked Nathan, his interest instantly piqued.

"Well, you remember me telling you we were going to get a technician to drain the hot tub to establish the cause of the accident? Well, we've just had his report and it turns out the sealed lights at the bottom of the tub had been deliberately tampered with to remove the safety mechanisms in the fittings. Whoever did it must have known that when it was refilled with water, it would become a likely death trap for anyone who stepped into it."

"And there's no way the damage could have occurred accidentally or as a result of wear and tear?" said Nathan.

"No way. The safety mechanisms in the bulbs incorporate some kind of cut-out that prevents this kind of thing from happening, and they'd all been disabled. I'm no electrician, so you'll forgive me if that isn't the correct terminology, but that's the gist of it. Long story short, the damage wasn't accidental.

"And when we examined the bulb casings we saw that all of them had identical indentations on them. It appears that a flat-bladed implement was used to prise the covers off and a search of the garden shed revealed a screwdriver, the shaft of which perfectly matches the indents.

"I must say, it surprised us to find the screwdriver on the premises, back in its box along with all the others in the set. We can only assume that whoever used it obviously didn't envisage it being discovered or linked to Mr Ingram's death, so didn't go to the trouble of disposing of it. I should stress, it may be that *none* of the people who were present at the time of Mr Ingram's death are responsible, but we're equally keen to eliminate suspects from our enquiries as we are to find the perpetrator."

"So you want the DNA samples to match what was found on the screwdriver?"

"Exactly," said Toby.

Nathan suddenly recalled what Penny had said in London. "Are you aware that the day of the barbecue was the first time the hot tub was used during that particular visit to the house? That being the case, I find it hard to see how anyone had the time, or the privacy, to tamper with the tub without anyone else knowing about it, wouldn't you say?"

"Ah, well, a salient point which I forgot to mention, is that it appears the damage was done some considerable time *before* the recent visit to London, as was indicated by the amount of rust which had formed on the bulb casings," said Toby.

"Now, according to Penny Baker, she and her sister are very generous in allowing their friends to use the place whenever they want to, and Owen Fisher said he was sure they'd all visited at some point during the past year. He also said that, as far as he was aware, there had been no problems with the hot tub on any of the previous visits.

"As I said, it may be that none of them are guilty of any wrongdoing—it's quite feasible that a complete stranger could have gained access to the garden and tampered with the hot tub—but I'm keeping an open mind."

"I see," said Nathan. "Well, I have to say, I'm surprised that any of them would want to cause the others harm. I only met them briefly, of course, but they seemed to be genuinely close friends. Then again, who knows what grudges they may be holding?"

"Very true, Nathan, very true. Anyway, if you're around tomorrow, we'll drop by before we travel back up the motorway."

"I'm around all day, Toby. Look forward to seeing you then."

As he put down the phone, Nathan hoped that Charlotte didn't find out about the latest development in the Frankie Ingram case.

The last thing she needed was stress, and the news Toby Carter had just shared with him would only serve to raise her anxiety levels.

This was one piece of information he would definitely be keeping to himself.

oooooooo

"I can't tell you on what the DNA sample was found, only that we've been able to ascertain foul play and we have reason to believe that the person from whom the sample came *may* have been involved in causing the accident."

Fighting for space with a chocolate Labrador and a scruffy mongrel, Toby Carter tried to find a cool spot to stand in Penny and Owen's sunlight-flooded kitchen.

"Well, I'm telling you right now, you've wasted your time coming all the way down here," said Penny. "It won't be any of us who fiddled with the hot tub. None of us wished Frankie any harm—we loved him. God, just the thought of it makes me feel sick. Who would be twisted enough to do something like that?" She paced the tiled floor, a deep furrow at her brow.

"None of us would *ever* do anything to hurt each other. I'm offended that you'd even insinuate one of us might be to blame—you should be out looking for whoever *is* responsible, not wasting time here with us."

"Miss Baker." An enthusiastic DS Rafferty took a swab from a sealed pack. "We don't only use DNA results to incriminate, you know. They're equally helpful in ascertaining who should be *eliminated* from our enquiries, which is precisely why our time here today is not, in the slightest, being wasted." He flashed a smile at Penny before turning to Amy. "Right, your turn now. If you can open wide, please."

"Hold on a second," said Owen. "Isn't it possible that *everything* at the house will have our DNA on it? It's our house, after all. What happens then?"

"Well, if that's the case, we'll look for corroborative evidence to remove any doubt, but we'll cross that bridge when we come to it, Mr Fisher. Whatever our investigations bring to light, I can assure you, we're not in the habit of locking people up on a whim," DI Carter allowed himself a brief smile, "whatever you may have heard to the contrary."

"Well, I'm telling you, whoever did this is a stranger and I won't set foot back in that house again until you have them under lock and key." Penny wagged her finger at the detectives. "It'll be bad enough going back there anyway, after what happened to Frankie, but knowing that someone *deliberately* rigged the hot tub to cause us harm is beyond belief." She shook her head. "So what are you doing about finding some *real* suspects?"

Toby Carter held up his hands. "Now, hold on. We don't know for sure that this is personal. Unfortunately, there are some strange people out there who carry out these random acts of vandalism for fun with no regard for the consequences. Empty holiday homes are often the target for all kinds of criminal activity.

"And we've already checked the DNA collected at the scene against our database and there are no matches so, whoever's responsible is not known to us. Don't worry, though, Miss Baker, we won't give up until we've found the perpetrator."

"Thank goodness that's over with." Amy shivered as she watched DS Rafferty drop a cotton swab into a tube and fasten the lid. She ran her fingers through her hair. "I still haven't come to terms with what happened and this has brought it all up again. It could have been *me* who got in that tub. It could have been any one of us."

"Sorry you've been caused distress, Miss Baker, but you'll understand that we have to be as thorough as possible." Toby Carter took his notebook from the inside pocket of his beige mac. "Now, if we can just take a sample from you, Mr Fisher, and then I'd like to ask you a few questions, if I may?"

"More questions?" Owen frowned. "I would have thought we'd answered enough already." He peered into Zac's cot. "Okay, but can we keep the noise down? I'd rather he didn't wake up just yet."

"Won't take long, Mr Fisher, and yes, of course, we'll keep it down. I just need clarification on a few more things that have come to light since we last met. Now then, Miss Baker, can you confirm exactly who has used the property since the last time you were all there together, which I think you said was in," the detective looked back in his notebook, "June of last year? And also, who was the last person, or persons, to stay at the house, prior to Mr Ingram's death?"

"Well, I'm pretty sure we've all used the house during the past year, haven't we, Owen?" Penny nodded, then stopped and shook her head. "Oh, no. Wait, I'm not sure about Aidan and Ruby. No, they *were* going to visit and then they cancelled. And Aidan wasn't there for last year's Internat Tat Awards, either. That would mean the last people to use it were Owen and me in February."

"And you used the hot tub during your visit?"

Penny nodded. "We use the tub every time we go to the house, except for the rare occasion we're on a flying visit and don't have time to get it set up. But the last time we were there, yes, we did."

"And that was in February, you say?" Toby Carter's illegible scrawl filled the pages of his notebook.

"Yes, that's right."

"I see. So, what would you say if I told you that someone has reported seeing a man and woman at the house in March? No description of the man, but we understand the woman may have been blonde." He stopped writing and stared intently at Penny.

"In March? I'd say they were mistaken. No one visited after us." Penny looked to Owen for confirmation. "Did they?"

"No. We were definitely the last."

"Oh, for goodness' sake!" Amy threw her arms up. "I bet it was Elsie Rayner who told you someone was at the house, wasn't it?" She shook her head in disbelief.

"Have you *seen* the lenses on her glasses? She's so short-sighted, they're like double-glazed windows. And until she gets that cataract sorted out, I doubt she could see two foot in front of her, let alone two doors down. And as for giving an accurate description of someone she claims to have seen from that distance…well, all in all, I'd say she's not the most reliable of witnesses."

"But a witness all the same, Miss Baker, and we have to take all statements into account." Toby closed his notebook and nodded to his colleague. "Right, we've finished for now. Thanks again for your time."

"What do you mean you've finished 'for now'?" Amy frowned.

"Just that, Miss Baker. If we need to speak to you again, we'll be in touch. Right, we'll see ourselves out. Good day to you all."

ooooooo

"Is there really any need for this?" Aidan Pitt strode around his living room, a vein in the side of his forehead throbbing. "I take it you remember who we are or, at least, who *I* am?"

Ignoring his question, Toby Carter cleared his throat. "At this point, Mr Pitt, we are merely trying to establish who are the persons of interest in this investigation, and who are not, and the DNA samples will assist us in establishing that. I assume you wish to be eliminated from our investigation?"

"Of course I do!" A little less full of bluster, Aidan sat down on the couch next to his wife, who placed her hand on his thigh in a gesture of solidarity.

"So, you believe the accident was planned?" A frown robbed Ruby's face of its smile. "I can't believe it. I just can't believe anyone would do that intentionally. Can you, Aidan?"

"What? No, I suppose not." He drummed his fingers against the arm of the couch.

"Well, we don't *know* that it was planned—it could have been a random act—but we do know that the damage was caused intentionally," said Toby. "Now all we have to do is find out by whom, and their motive."

"Alright, alright," huffed Aidan. "Well, can we get on with it? I'm sure you have other things you'd rather be doing—I know I have."

"And what happens once you've found the person who matches the DNA you found at the house?" asked Ruby as DS Rafferty produced an swab for her sample.

"We'll need to determine whether they actually were involved, or whether there's a valid reason for their DNA being present. If we need to contact either you or your husband again once we have the test results, you'll be the first to know."

"Well, let's hope that doesn't happen. I'll show you out." Aidan marched to the front door, his mouth set in a thin line.

"That must be our cue to leave," said Toby, shaking hands with Ruby.

"Sorry about Aidan," she said. "I'm sure he doesn't mean to be so rude."

"Don't worry, Mrs Pitt," said Toby. "We're quite used to it in our line of work."

ooooooo

"Listen, you don't need to take a sample to eliminate me from your enquiries." Eddie Lewis chewed on his thumbnail. "I'm telling you, there's no way I could have tampered with that hot tub for three very good reasons.

He counted on his fingers. "Number one, Frankie was like a brother to me. Number two, I wouldn't wish harm on any of the people who were there on the day he died—I love them all to death. And number three, I work for Aidan Pitt all the hours God sends. I barely get time to visit my mother, who's only a three-hour drive away, let alone to drive five and a half hours to London and back again. Aidan will vouch for me—I hardly ever take time off."

"Regardless of that, Mr Lewis, we'd be obliged if you'd consider agreeing to give a sample voluntarily. If you've done nothing wrong, you have nothing to worry about."

Eddie blew out a piece of nail and moved to his index finger. "I'm not under arrest, am I?"

Toby eyed the young man. "No, you're not under arrest."

"So you can't force me to give a sample, can you?"

"No. That's why we need your consent. But all we're trying to do is establish who was responsible for your friend's death—that's what we want the sample for. No other reason."

"It'll only take a second." DS Rafferty stood poised and ready to open the sealed pack containing the swab.

Eddie glowered at the detective, his pleasant face unusually grim. "And there's no chance you'll speak to Aidan or Ruby, so they can tell you I've never taken time off to travel to London on my own?"

Hamburgers, Homicide and a Honeymoon

"Not in lieu of a sample, no."

Eddie clicked the end of his pen repeatedly as he contemplated his decision. "Alright, I'll give the damn sample." He signed the form and slung the pen across the table. "But I'm not happy about it."

ooooooo

Toby Carter and Ken Rafferty were decidedly hot and bothered as Nathan ushered them into his air-conditioned office.

"Nice to see you both. Amanda, bring in some mineral water, would you? Thanks."

When Toby wiped his brow with a handkerchief, and droplets of perspiration dampened Ken's cropped hair, Nathan turned up the air conditioning for the benefit of his visibly wilting guests.

"Thank you." Toby gratefully accepted a bottle of iced mineral water, taking it from the tray that Amanda had placed on the desk and, foregoing the glass which sat beside it, removed the lid and drank it down in one long draught. "It was forty-nine degrees and raining when we left London this morning," he said, wiping his hand across his mouth. "I can't believe how hot it is here—it's like the bloody Costa del Sol."

"And not even the offer of a glass of water from anyone," said Ken, loosening his tie and unfastening his top button.

"So, how did you get on?" Nathan leaned back in his chair and regarded the perspiring detectives with amusement. "Was everyone agreeable to supplying you with a sample?"

"Well." Toby took off his coat and hung it over the back of his chair. "As you'd imagine, everyone denied

Page 91

culpability and were all suitably affronted that we'd asked. Everyone except Aidan and Ruby Pitt. Well, he was affronted, certainly, but he didn't immediately put up a defensive argument like the rest of them did. And Ruby Pitt, well, she didn't really get a chance to speak, but she didn't deny any involvement. Not that that means she's guilty of anything, it was just noticeable because everyone else was so keen to put themselves in the clear."

"And Mr Lewis' behaviour was a little strange, too, wasn't it, Guv?" Ken Rafferty's face had moved a couple of shades down the colour chart from crimson to dark pink.

Toby nodded. "It certainly was. He definitely did *not* want to give us a sample. Not at all. I thought we were going to leave empty-handed and have to come back again but he agreed, eventually. We wondered if he's committed other crimes in his past and he's concerned that the DNA results could connect him to them."

"Well, he's not familiar to the St. Eves force, so he's caused no problems here that I'm aware of," said Nathan. "Same goes for the rest of them. That said, if you need any help with the investigation that would be more expediently dealt with from here, just say the word if there's anything my officers or I can do to help."

Although his offer was sincere, Nathan hoped it wouldn't be taken up. There'd been enough murderers to deal with in St. Eves in recent years, and he hoped there wasn't another one in their midst.

CHAPTER 6

"Oh, come on, Charlotte!" said Ava. "Surely you could ask him to pop in for a cup of tea or something. And then Harriett and I could be sitting on another table, acting nonchalantly, of course, and you could introduce us. We could ask some of our acquaintances along—we know a group of women who are mad keen on Aidan Pitt, you know."

"Yes! I mean, it's not as though he'd think it was strange," said Harriett. "You *did* go on holiday together, after all."

The friends were doing their best to persuade Charlotte to set up a meeting between them and Aidan, a favour which she had no intention of carrying out.

"Er, I think he would find it *very* strange if I just called him out of the blue, because I barely know him," said Charlotte. "And we did *not* go on holiday together! We just happened to travel to London on the same plane. I don't even have his number—I met him once for about five minutes and, between you and me, I thought he was very standoffish. Anyway, sorry, the answer's no and I can't discuss it anymore because I've got things to do in the kitchen."

She was grateful to get away. There weren't many things she wouldn't do for Ava, Harriett or Betty, but this was definitely one of them.

"I think those women who came in the other day are walking up the marina." Jess stuck her head through the hole in the wall between the café and the kitchen and passed Charlotte three food tickets.

"What women?"

"The ones you met while you were in London.

"Well, if they're coming in here for a chat, can you let them know they'll have to wait, please? I've got food orders to get out."

Five minutes later, Jess was back. "No need for you to rush to get out there—Ava and Harriett are keeping them entertained."

Charlotte bashed a chicken breast flat with a rolling pin for a breaded escalope. "Alright, I'll pop out and say hello as soon as I've finished this."

Twenty minutes later, Charlotte went out to join Penny and Amy who were howling with laughter at Ava's account of her one and only visit to Harriett's yoga class.

"...and then I felt something go *ping*! Well, my dears, to begin with, I wasn't sure if it was my back or the Lycra in my yoga pants, but then I couldn't move. I like to think I'm quite flexible but, I can assure you, stuck in the lotus position for forty minutes is no laughing matter...not with a bladder like mine." She sniffed and stirred her coffee.

"Well, if only you'd said you were having problems with your back, that situation could have been so easily avoided." Harriett rolled her eyes as she filed a nail. "That's the trouble with Ava," she said to Penny and Amy. "She doesn't like people to think she can't do something, so she just throws herself into totally unsuitable situations and ends up coming off worst." She wagged her nail file in the air. "And don't give me that look, Ava Whittington, you know I'm right!"

Ava opened her mouth to retort but Charlotte stopped her in her tracks.

"Alright, ladies, that's enough, if you don't mind! This is only Penny and Amy's second visit and I'd like to think there'll be a third. I don't need you two playing fisticuffs and scaring the customers away, thank you very much."

She slowly lowered herself into a chair next to Penny. "Nice to see you again."

"Yes, nice to see you." Penny wiped her eyes. "Oh, I haven't laughed like that for ages. Those women are a riot! Are they regulars?"

Charlotte glanced over to Ava and Harriett, who were pretending they weren't listening. "Yes, they're part of the fixtures and fittings. If I ever sell this place, they'll be on the inventory. So, what are your plans for the rest of the day?"

Penny smiled. "Well, it was so nice here the other morning and it really helped to take our minds off things, we thought we'd come and see you again. Owen's looking after Zac, I'm up to date with all my assignments, and Amy still can't face going back to work at the tattoo shop, so we're treating ourselves to a bit of quality sister time. We're going to have a bite to eat here first, and then we're going to go and lie on the beach."

"Very nice, too," said Charlotte. "And how are you both?"

"Hmpf, after what happened this morning, shell-shocked," said Amy. "Those detectives from London came to see us. They said the hot tub was deliberately tampered with—something about the safety device on the bulbs being disabled—can you believe it? As if we're not already having a difficult enough time dealing with what happened."

"*What?*" said Charlotte, as her whole body tightened with anxiety. "That's terrible!"

"*And* they took DNA samples from all of us to match to some DNA they found at the house," Amy continued, "although I'm sure they don't really think it's any of us who's responsible. They said it's likely to have been vandals who target empty holiday homes and mess with stuff to make it dangerous. Unbelievable how some people get their kicks." She blew her nose.

"Anyway, they're going to be in touch," said Penny. "I don't know quite how it works but I've heard that DNA isn't always 100% accurate, so I'm a little apprehensive about the results."

"Well, you've got nothing to be concerned about, have you? I mean, it's not like you've done anything wrong?" Charlotte rubbed the small of her back to ease a twinge.

"No, of course not, but you hear stories about people being wrongly accused of things, don't you. It's a little disconcerting, that's all." Penny twisted a thick silver band on her wedding ring finger and shuddered.

"Oh, and you'll never guess. You remember Elsie Rayner, our nosy neighbour in London? Well, she told the police she saw a man and a woman with blonde hair at the house in March. Like she'd be able to see anything that specific through those glasses of hers. Anyway, she's definitely mistaken because no one was at the house in March. She's a bloody troublemaker, that woman. Ooh, it makes me mad just thinking about her—let's change the subject to something less irritating."

"You know what?" said Amy. "I would love to have been a fly on the wall when the police called round at Aidan and Ruby's—you know what he's like! I bet he was furious. I'm sure he thinks the justice system exists for everyone except him. It must have been a real shock for him to be treated like a mere mortal for a change!"

Suddenly even more aware of Ava and Harriett sitting at the next table, surreptitiously leaning over as they pretended not to be listening to the conversation, Charlotte decided it was a good time to get back to work.

"Well, I'm sure it'll all work out—one way or another—and I'm so glad to see you looking a little happier. It's been lovely seeing you again but I've got a lot to be getting on with. Don't forget the baby shower on Saturday if you can make it. No pressure, of course, but you're more than welcome. Right, I'll leave you to order your food. Maybe see you on Saturday."

ooooooo

After they'd closed the café, Charlotte took a walk into town with Jess to buy some last-minute party favours for the baby shower.

"What sort of thing are you looking for?"

"Well, I was thinking of getting some of those small satin bags from the gift shop—you know, the small ones with the drawstring—and filling them with a selection of old-fashioned sweets."

"So I take it we're going to Crunchies, then?"

Selling every imaginable type of sweet, Crunchies was the oldest sweet shop in the county. Jar upon jar filled with all manner of confections lined the shelves and, for over a century, generations of the same family had welcomed thousands of customers through the doors.

Large cabinets with glass fronts housed the larger sweets—foot-long candy-striped walking canes, large pink and white sugar mice, and giant jelly snakes—and their random placement within the shop resulted in a slightly higgledy-piggledy appearance which only added to its charm.

Charlotte and Jess made their way down the narrow, cobbled high street past the bakery, the waterfront pubs, the coffee bars, and the antique and art shops. At the bottom of the high street was the old sweet shop with the pink frontage, and pink and white candy-striped awning that kept the sun off the window display of homemade sweets from a bygone age.

As they were about to go inside, Charlotte spotted a familiar face. "Ruby? Ruby, hi! It's me, Charlotte…from London."

The woman's vacant expression was replaced by a brief smile of acknowledgement. "Oh, yes, hi. Good to see you."

"You, too. Jess, this is Ruby Pitt. She was in London with her husband. Ruby, this is my friend, Jess."

"Nice to meet you." The women nodded to each other.

"So, um, how are you?" said Charlotte, suddenly feeling a little awkward.

Ruby shrugged. "Oh, you know…been better. I still can't get my head around the fact that I'll never see Frankie again—none of us can. It's such an awful feeling. And we had the most horrible visit from the police this afternoon." She shivered, despite the warmth of the early evening sun. "Anyway, how're things with you?"

"Good, thanks. I'm just doing a bit of last-minute shopping for my baby shower."

Ruby pulled a face. "What, in Crunchies?"

Charlotte nodded. "Yes. Don't you like sweets?"

"I love them," said Ruby, "but that shop makes me itch. I went in once and couldn't wait to get out again. The layout's a nightmare and everything's all over the place—there's no order. You probably won't understand but it makes me feel anxious."

"But that's part of its charm, don't you think?" said Jess. "It's like stepping back in time when you go in there, just like the shops we used to go in when we were kids."

"My point exactly," said Ruby, scratching her arm. "See, I'm getting hives just thinking about it. I've got OCD," she said in response to the puzzled looks she was getting from Charlotte and Jess. "It's not severe but it's bad enough to make me feel uncomfortable if I set foot over the threshold of that shop.

"The only time I went in there, all I wanted to do was tidy everything up, group all the sweets by colour, and straighten all the jars so the labels faced the front. Aidan thinks I'm crazy but I can't help it—I get it from my dad. He's always said, 'A place for everything and everything in its place.' He drummed it into my siblings and me as kids and now, if I see anything out of place or untidy, it freaks me out a little. Even mild OCD can be very controlling."

"Oh, I see," said Charlotte. "Well, you definitely won't want to come inside then but if you'd like to come to the baby shower, you're welcome to tag along with Penny and Amy. It's on Saturday."

"Saturday?" said Ruby. "I'm not sure I'll be able to make it but I'll certainly try." She looked at her watch. "Well, I must fly. I've got a million things to do. Nice to meet you, Jess."

"So that's Ruby Pitt?" Jess watched as she retreated down the high street.

"Yes. She seems quite nice but I couldn't help feel a bit sorry for her in London." Charlotte peered at a jar filled with iridescent baubles which the label confirmed were Fruit Glow Rainbow Drops. "Aidan didn't pay her much attention that I noticed, and it was pretty obvious. If she comes to the baby shower, I think she'll be good fun on her own."

"Well, I hope so," muttered Jess. "Sorry, but the last thing you need is her moping about her dead friend all afternoon, isn't it? Same goes for the other two. I don't mean to sound harsh—I know they're all really upset—but it's a baby shower, not a wake. It's supposed to be a happy occasion. You know, when we look forward to welcoming the little one, and I'd hate for anything to ruin it for you." She put her arm around Charlotte and rested her head on her shoulder.

"Well, I appreciate the sentiment," said Charlotte, "but, to be honest, I doubt that any of them will turn up so I don't think they'll be ruining anything any time soon." Her mouth fell open as a vast jar filled with face-sized pinwheel lollipops caught her eye.

"You know what, though? I think I might need to rethink the size of the drawstring bags…"

ooooooo

"I had a very interesting conversation today." Charlotte kicked off her flip-flops and sank her feet into the cool, recently watered lawn.

"Did you, now? And who might that have been with?" Nathan turned the hose onto the yellow and white blooms of the Charlotte rose bush in the corner of the garden, a present from Garrett and Laura for Charlotte's last birthday.

"Penny and Amy." She waited to see Nathan's response but, apart from nodding as he unwound some more hose from the reel, there was none.

"Were you ever going to tell me that six St. Eves residents are possible suspects in Frankie Ingram's death? *Six!*" Her voice increased in pitch.

"Now listen." Nathan turned off the hose and guided her into a garden chair. "You can't honestly wonder why I didn't say anything. I mean, if there was ever a queen of stress I know who'd be wearing the crown.

"I know you probably would have found out sooner or later—you know what this place is like, nothing stays secret for long—but I didn't see the point in worrying you about it. Not in your condition."

"Listen, Nathan, when *you* give me bad news, you make sure I'm in a relaxed environment, and you tell me in a way that doesn't send my stress levels through the roof," said Charlotte. "It's when I hear it from someone else who just blurts it out that it's likely to send me into a mild panic. Which it did."

Nathan crouched down and took hold of her hands. "You're right—I should have told you, but Toby Carter only told me yesterday and it didn't even occur to me that you'd find out so soon. I'm sorry."

She shook her head. "It's okay. It's not your fault—it's me. I know I worry about everything far too much. I wish I didn't but I can't help it." She smiled. "But seeing as I know now, you might as well tell me what's going on."

Nathan recounted what Toby Carter had told him.

"That's interesting. I wonder why the screwdriver that was used to damage the hot tub was left behind—why wouldn't whoever did it have taken it with them? And why was Eddie reluctant to give a DNA sample, I wonder? It doesn't make him look very good, does it?" Charlotte threw a ball for Pippin and he ran after it, tumbling over and over on the grass before catching it deftly between his teeth.

"Not really, although there are lots of people who don't like giving DNA, or even fingerprints. They see it as a violation of their civil rights. I've no idea if that's why Eddie didn't want to give a sample but, if he's innocent, that could be the reason. Of course, the other reason may be that he knows DNA isn't always 100% accurate. That could be a concern."

"Hmm, maybe that's why Aidan wasn't keen," said Charlotte. "What did the DI say about the couple the neighbour claims to have seen?"

"What couple?"

"Amy said a neighbour told the police she saw some people at the house in March. You remember the woman who came round with the cat when we were there?"

"Really? That's news to me." Nathan resumed watering the flowerbeds.

"It was a man and a blonde woman, apparently," said Charlotte. "But no one went to the house in March so the neighbour obviously didn't see what she thought she saw."

"Well, whatever the situation, it's nothing for you to worry about," said Nathan. "I don't want you getting your knickers in a twist about something that's absolutely nothing to do with you. Okay? Promise me?"

Charlotte pushed herself up from the chair. "I can't promise I'm not going to worry but I promise I'll try—how's that for you?"

Nathan winked. "That'll do for now."

ooooooo

Charlotte fumbled in the dark for the alarm clock. 5:56 am.

It was no good. She couldn't sleep. Her mind was too active.

Something was troubling her.

Since she and Nathan had returned to St. Eves, it had become increasingly difficult for her to switch off. Nathan was convinced it was because of the baby but she knew otherwise.

There was something about Frankie's death that bothered her. Apart from the fact that he'd been electrocuted in a hot tub, of course.

She'd gone over everything that had happened time and time again but she was missing something—she knew it.

She just didn't know what it was.

She swung her legs off the side of the bed and waited for the baby to settle itself before creeping downstairs to make her go-to insomnia cure—hot milk and maple syrup—Pippin scampering ahead.

Sitting at the kitchen table, she pulled a writing pad and pen from underneath a pile of newspapers, and started making notes.

The bulbs in the hot tub had been deliberately tampered with, rendering it a death trap as soon as it was filled with water and switched on.

But who was the culprit?

A screwdriver which had been used to affect the damage had been found at the scene with traces of DNA on it.

But why hadn't the perpetrator taken it with them, instead of putting it back where it came from? Why would they leave such a huge clue behind?

Who could have gained access to the garden and made the deadly alterations?

The neighbour had said she'd seen a man and a woman with blonde hair at the house at a time when none of the group who fitted that description could possibly have been there. But how reliable was her recollection of events?

Charlotte recalled the lenses on the woman's glasses had been thicker than the bottom of a milk bottle. She was doubtful she could have made a positive identification of anyone.

It was unsettling, to say the least, to think that one of the group could have been responsible—unbelievable, too.

She didn't know any of them well, but she was usually a pretty good judge of character and none of them struck her as a cold-blooded murderer.

She drank the last of her milk and washed up her cup. As she climbed the stairs, she tried to clear her mind of thoughts that would keep her from sleep but, later, as she tossed and turned and lay wide awake, she knew she'd failed.

CHAPTER 7

"Yoo-hoo, anyone home?" Ava's shrill voice called through the letter box at *Fisherman's Cottage*, Charlotte's cosy, seafront home.

"Hang on, I won't be a sec." Charlotte plumped up the cushions on the couch and checked her reflection in the mirror. In an effort to be as comfortable as possible, she'd pulled on a stretchy t-shirt dress, emphasising her ever-growing bump, which she patted proprietorially before answering the door.

"Hello, Charlotte, you look adorable, dear." Ava looked her up and down and patted her cheek with her free hand, the other carrying a large handbag and an even larger cakebox. "And hello, Pippin, sweetie."

"Yes, pregnancy really does agree with you, you're positively glowing," said Harriett, kissing her on both cheeks. She followed Ava into the kitchen. "By the way, I've made an apple and blackberry crumble."

"And I've made some homemade ice cream to go with it," said Betty. "I hope you're not on a diet."

"No, I'm most definitely not on a diet," said Charlotte. "Thanks, all of you. You didn't have to go to all this trouble."

And then, without warning, she burst into tears.

"Oh, I'm so sorry!" she took the tissue Jess shoved under her nose. "It's just…"

"Hormones!" chorused Jess, Ava, Harriett, and Betty, and Charlotte laughed through her tears.

"Don't worry about it, dear," said Ava from the depths of one of Charlotte's kitchen cupboards, her bottom stuck in the air and her head and shoulders out of sight.

"What are you looking for, Ava?" Charlotte dried her eyes and grinned at Ava's muttering as she rifled through the shelves of pots and pans.

"A cake stand. Honestly, youngsters these days and their awful habit of cutting a cake straight out of the packet. Don't tell me you don't have one?"

"I do, but it's not in there. It's in the cupboard above the fridge. I'll get it."

Ava broke down the sides of the box to reveal a fruit cake, its rich aroma fruity and spicy in equal measures.

"Mmmm, that smells divine—like Christmas cake." Charlotte helped Ava transfer the cake onto the stand.

"Hmm, similar, but not so heavy. It's a boiled fruit cake—my Grandma Doris's recipe." Ava ferreted in her vast bag and pulled a canister of icing sugar from its depths. "There," she said, with a flourish, one arm striking a chef-like pose as she sprinkled the surface of the cake liberally. "If you taste a better fruit cake than that, which I doubt, I want the recipe."

Pippin, who was sitting beside the cupboard, nose twitching, wasn't expecting to be sprinkled with icing sugar and Charlotte laughed as he suddenly shook himself and licked the sugar from his paws. "Well, it looks lovely. It all does. Thank you," she said, hugging them all.

"And we've got you some presents," said Ava. "We chose them between us so whenever you look at them, you can think of all of us."

"Yes, it took us ages to decide which ones to get." Betty beamed at Charlotte.

"But I think we definitely made the right choices in the end." Harriett busied herself arranging food on the kitchen table. "I'm sure you'll love them."

"Oh, you shouldn't have! But thank you—and yes, I'm sure I'll love them, whatever they are."

"We'll wait until everyone's here before we give them to you, though," said Ava, pulling up her cuff to look at her watch. "Now, where is everyone?"

oooooo

It wasn't long before the living room was filled with the sound of chatter and uproarious laughter.

As was so often the case, Ava and Harriett were keeping the guests entertained—on this occasion, with hilarious anecdotes of childbirth in years gone by—and Charlotte, Jess, Laura, Lola, Betty, Yolanda from the Maxi-Mart, Penny, Amy, and Ruby were soon helpless with laughter.

"Oh, Charlotte, this afternoon has done me the world of good." Amy wiped her eyes and checked her mascara.

"Well, in that case, I'm so glad you could make it," said Charlotte. "I wasn't sure you would."

"Well, after the last couple of weeks, we were both in dire need of some light relief," said Amy. "Weren't we, Pen?"

"You can say that again." Penny helped herself to a second slice of fruit cake. "It's so nice to just be able to focus on something else for a few hours in such lovely company."

"It really is," agreed Ruby, scratching Pippin behind the ears. "The last two weeks have been absolutely horrendous but this has been a real tonic. Honestly, I didn't think I'd ever laugh again after what happened in London."

"Speaking of which," said Amy as she licked a tissue and wiped away the mascara smudges from under her eyes, "we're having a Celebration of Life for Frankie next Saturday afternoon. It's the day of his funeral but, as we're not invited, we wanted to remember him in our own way."

"Oh. Why aren't you invited?" said Charlotte.

"Because we found out yesterday that his family wants a private service—family only. We're devastated because Frankie knew so many people who'd love to go and pay their respects." Penny popped the last piece of cake into her mouth. "Anyway, we'd be thrilled if you'd come along. And Nathan, too, of course. I remember you saying that you can't usually go to anything unless it's on a Saturday, so you're in luck!"

"Well, we hardly knew him," said Charlotte. "I'm not sure we'd feel comfortable about intruding on something so personal."

"Don't be daft! You wouldn't be intruding. And it's a celebration—a party—so the more, the merrier. We want to give him the best send-off we can. Anyway, you don't know *us* very well but you invited us to your baby shower, didn't you? That's personal, isn't it?"

"Um, yes, I suppose it is. Okay, I'll mention it to Nathan and I'll let you know, if that's okay? Thanks for the invite."

"Well, if he can't make it, bring your friend, Jess, along if you want to. She seems lovely."

"Charlotte! It's time!" Ava clapped her hands to attract everyone's attention. "It's time for the first part of your present! Now, Harriett, Betty, and I gave a lot of thought about what we could give you that was different from any other present you'd receive. We wanted to give you something personal that you would always remember us by, didn't we, ladies?"

"We did. Something unique." Harriett nodded.

"Yes, and useful, too." Betty's eyes twinkled as she beamed at Charlotte.

"So, everyone follow us! Outside into the garden! Come along!" The three women marched towards the back door, Pippin bringing up the rear.

"What?" Charlotte was bemused. "There's nothing *in* the garden. I was out there this morning hanging out the washing. I would have seen it if there was."

"Yes, there is, dear. Nathan collected it from my place a few days ago and put it in the garden shed while you were at work. It's been there ever since." Ava opened the back door and waited for Charlotte to file out with the others. "And don't look so surprised. He's been in on this from the beginning. It was him who suggested the shed would be a good place to keep it because you never go in there. Now come along."

They gathered on the patio and Jess and Laura rushed forward to help Betty and Harriett push a large gift-wrapped box out of the shed.

"Come on, Charlotte. Come and open your first present," said her three friends, looking extremely pleased with themselves.

"I can't believe Nathan managed to keep this a secret." Charlotte ripped wrapping paper off the package, carefully opened the lid of the box and peered inside.

"Oh. Oh, my!" She tore open the sides of the cardboard box to reveal a beautiful, brightly decorated, solid wood child's rocking horse.

Pippin took one look at it, cocked his head, and began to bark, madly chasing his tail.

"It's an antique, you know—fully restored," said Ava, excitedly.

"All handmade and hand-painted," said Betty.

"And it's just like the rocking horses Ava and I had for our little ones—so much nicer than the ones in the shops these days. These have so much character, don't you think?" said Harriet, squeezing Charlotte's hand.

All three women looked suddenly hesitant. "You do like it, don't you?" said Ava.

A smile lit up Charlotte's face. "*Like* it? I adore it! Thank you so much, it's such a generous gift."

"Oh, get away with you." Ava swiped playfully at Charlotte. "What did you think we were going to give you? A crocheted bib and booties, and a tube of teething gel? Do give us some credit, dear."

"Shall I fetch the other gift?" said Betty. Without waiting for an answer she disappeared inside, reappearing with a package wrapped in brown paper which she pushed into Charlotte's hand. "Go on, open it! We haven't had a chance to look at it yet because it was only delivered this morning but I'm sure it'll be fine."

"Oh, thank you, it's so sweet of you." Charlotte tore at the paper . Really, there was no need to—oh, it's very yellow, isn't it?" The package contained something soft and bright yellow. She unfolded the garment and held it by the shoulders.

"Don't you just love it?" said Harriett.

"It's a 1960s-design maternity dress! Just like the ones Harriett and I used to wear!" Ava looked about to burst with excitement.

"They chose the style and I chose the colour!" said Betty.

"We had it made especially for you!" said Harriett. "You know, to keep you covered up."

"Yes, much better than those dreadful things pregnant women wear these days, showing off their belly button—honestly!" Ava lowered her voice to a whisper when she said 'belly button' as if it was a profanity.

"Actually, Ava, it looks a little long, don't you think?" Harriett sized up the garment through a squint.

As Charlotte wordlessly held out the giant yellow dress in front of her, Jess caught her eye.

"Well, if Big Bird ever comes looking for his coat, at least we'll be able to tell him where to find it." Her voice quavered as she suppressed the giggles that were threatening to erupt.

"Oh, shush, Jess. Don't tell her that, you'll give her a complex," said Betty.

"Well? Aren't you going to try it on?" Ava's tone told Charlotte that she'd get no rest until she did.

"Of course she's going to try it on!" said Harriett. "Aren't you?"

"Oh yes, *please* try it on, Charlotte!" A handful of tissues caught Laura's silent tears of mirth.

"Yes, yes, you must!" Lola's face was a picture as she struggled to hold back the giggles.

"I'll try it on later." Charlotte smiled gratefully and put the dress back into its bag.

"Nonsense! You'll try it on now! Just slip it on over your clothes," said Ava. "I think it'll be roomy enough."

To the sound of ill-concealed splutters and thinly-veiled attempts to disguise strangled laughter as coughing, Charlotte lifted the garment over her head.

"There we are, perfect!" The three women stood back to admire their gift.

The capacious dress hung from Charlotte's shoulders and fell two inches above her ankles, its girth more than capable of housing three pregnant women at once.

She glared at Jess, Laura, and Lola—as ridiculous as she knew she must look, she would hate for Ava, Harriett, and Betty's feelings to be hurt. She didn't want anyone laughing at her in front of them.

"Hmmm." Ava frowned as she gathered a handful of excess material. "I see what you mean, Harriett. It *is* a little on the large side, isn't it? I wonder why?"

"You did give the measurements in centimetres on the order form, didn't you, not inches?" asked Harriett.

Ava blushed before changing the subject. "Ahem. Well, a maternity dress can never be too loose, if you ask me."

Sensing her embarrassment, Charlotte held out the skirt of the voluminous yellow dress and did a little twirl. "It's lovely. Thank you all—you're very kind."

An awkward silence was broken by Betty.

"That reminds me... I haven't heard the church bells ringing recently. Is one of them missing?" Her mischievous comment, in her kindly voice, was all that was needed to reduce Jess, Laura, and Lola to quivering wrecks, helpless with laughter, with everyone else following suit soon afterwards.

"Oh, my gosh, I ache!" Charlotte hid her face in the skirt of her dress. "You shouldn't make a pregnant woman laugh so much! Please stop, or I'll embarrass myself—you know I'm not in control of all my functions at the moment, what with all this extra weight making me want to run to the bathroom every five minutes."

"Well, if it's extra weight you're worried about, you'd better take that dress off," said Harriett. "They must have used a ton of fabric to make it!"

ooooooo

"So, your husband doesn't mind all your tattoos?"

"No, not at all. He sees them as body art."

Ruby had been fielding questions from Ava and Harriett for the past fifteen minutes.

"Not that *I* mind them, you understand," said Ava. "I'm very up with the new trends, you see. No, dear, it's just that the one on the back of your leg is rather large, isn't it? I can't say I've ever seen a tattoo of a bunch of purple orchids before, but there's a first time for everything, I suppose. Has anyone ever mistaken it for a bruise?"

"Er, no." Ruby grinned. "Not yet, anyway."

"Well, as I've already said, I think they're rather eye-catching but others might say they were…er, how can I put it without offending, my dear…a little unbecoming on a woman, shall we say?"

"Well, Aidan doesn't object to them at all," said Ruby. "He quite likes them, in fact."

Ava's face took on the expression that Charlotte had seen many times. It was the expression that told you she didn't believe a word you were saying.

"Anyway, let's change the subject," said Ava. "Tell us, dear, how did you and Aidan meet?"

Ava and Harriett could hardly contain themselves to be attending a party at which their heartthrob's wife was one of the guests. "Cindy and Brenda are going to be green with envy when we tell them. We must get some selfies," Ava had whispered to Harriett earlier, "or they'll never believe us."

"Well, it's not a very exciting story," said Ruby. "I'm sure you don't want to hear it."

"On the contrary, my dear, we absolutely do. Hold on for just a second, though."

Ava plonked herself down on the couch next to a startled Ruby, her face fixed with a manic grin, and stuck her thumb in the air. Nudging Ruby in the ribs she said, "Say cheese, dear—Harriett, take it now! *Now*, Harriett! Right, carry on, dear." As if nothing had happened, she moved back to her chair and assumed an attentive pose.

"Erm, right... well, I was Aidan's programme researcher when he worked for the TV station. We knew each other for a couple of years before we even went on a date. I suppose I never considered him in a romantic way because he was my boss and he was quite a bit older than me.

"Anyway, we were working late one night and when we left the office, he invited me to join him for a bite to eat. He said that buying me dinner was the least he could do for keeping me so late. And that's where it all started. Ruby laughed. "See, I told you it wasn't very exciting."

"Not being rude but wasn't he married when you got together?" Betty spooned a mouthful of blackberry and apple crumble and ice cream into her mouth.

"*Betty!*" said Charlotte, with an eye roll.

"No, please don't worry, it's okay." Ruby smiled and nodded. "Yes, he was, but he'd been living apart from his wife for a long time. She wouldn't file for divorce on religious grounds and he just never got around to it so they stayed married, but estranged, for years. Of course, when *we* decided to get married, he had to push for a divorce. We had a small ceremony in my hometown—very low-key—and that's about all there is to tell, really."

"Oh, how romantic!" Ava clasped her hands over her heart. "And tell me, dear, what's he *really* like? I mean, behind closed doors? Is he as delightful as we all imagine him to be? Harriett and I are very good friends with the founding members of 'The Pittettes', you know, and those who are lucky enough to have met him all say he's an absolute charmer."

Ruby smiled. "Well, he has his off days but, generally, yes, he's quite the ladies' man. To be honest, I didn't quite know what to make of 'The Pittettes' when I first heard about them. It still strikes me as a bit weird that Aidan has his own little fan club but I've met a few members myself and they've all been very nice. I've been jostled a few times while they've been trying to get to Aidan for an autograph but, otherwise, they've been very kind to me. And it's amazing how knowledgeable they are about Aidan's life—some of them remember more about it than he does!"

"Fascinating" said Ava. "I can only hope that we have the honour of meeting the great man ourselves one day."

"Well, I'll tell him you're a fan." Ruby patted Ava's hand. "I know he'll be delighted."

"Owwwwwww!" A cry of pain from Charlotte brought the conversation to an abrupt halt, prompting Jess, Laura, and Lola to rush to her side immediately.

"What is it? What's wrong?" said Laura, pushing Charlotte's hair back off her face.

"Owwwwwww! Oooh, I don't know. I've had a twinge in my back for a while and it suddenly got worse."

"A *while!* How long's a while?" Lola caught her niece's hand in a vice-like grip.

"A week or so, maybe a bit longer. I thought it was wind."

"Should I call an ambulance?" Jess's wide eyes were anxious.

"Is she having contractions?" said Harriett.

"Do you think that's what it is, love?" asked Laura

"I don't know. I've never had one before, but the pain's moving around to my stomach," said Charlotte, her face pinched with pain.

"Yes, Jess, get the ambulance," said Laura, taking her phone from her back pocket, "and I'll call Nathan."

"Look, I'm sure it's nothing to worry about…owwwww! Please don't feel like you have to go home, everyone, the party only just got going and there's so much food and drink." Charlotte forced a smile. "Stay and enjoy yourself, I'm sure I'll be back soon and I don't

Hamburgers, Homicide and a Honeymoon

want to come back to an empty house. Owwwww! I just need someone to come in the ambulance with me and someone to stay here and look after everyone till I get back."

"I'll come with you," Jess, Laura, Lola, and Ava all spoke at the same time.

"Oh, please don't make me pick one of you. Just choose someone...owwwww!"

"Right, there's only one fair way to do this. Scissors, paper, stone." Jess started the selection process and it took less than a minute to decide that Laura would go in the ambulance with Charlotte.

"It's here!" Ruby ran to open the door and Charlotte was soon being tended to by the medical personnel.

"Okay, Charlotte, we're going to take you to hospital for a check-up." A kindly paramedic with a soothing voice removed the blood pressure sleeve from Charlotte's arm.

"Is the baby okay?" Her voice wobbled and she bit her lip.

"Everything looks fine. We just want to be sure." The paramedic reassured her.

"Nathan's going to meet us there." Laura grabbed her bag and gave a tearful Jess a quick hug. "Don't worry, they'll look after her—I'm sure it's nothing serious. I'll call you when there's any news, okay?"

The door slammed and they were gone, leaving a room full of silence behind them.

"Well, I don't know about anyone else," said Jess, "but the last thing I feel like doing is having a party." She flopped onto the couch and began picking at her cuticles.

"I'm sure there's nothing to worry about, love." Lola sat next to Jess and squeezed her hand, although the expression on her face contradicted her words.

"I knew I should have told Nathan about the pains she's been having," said Jess, "but she told me not to worry."

"Look, you're not to blame—when I spoke to her a few days ago she told me she was getting twinges—*I* should have mentioned it to Nathan but I didn't," said Lola.

"Well, I hope to God she'll be okay. If anything happens to her, I'll never forgive myself," said Jess.

"Oh, for goodness' sake! Will you two harbingers of doom please *stop*!" Ava clamped her hands over her ears. "You heard what the paramedic said, didn't you? Everything looked fine and they just wanted to check Charlotte over at the hospital to be sure." She put her hands on her hips.

"Now, where's your fighting spirit? We won't do Charlotte any good at all if we mope around. We need to raise our energy levels and send her some positive thoughts and we can't do that if we're miserable—it's a physical impossibility."

"She's right, you know." Harriett flicked through the CD collection. "*20 Sing-Along, Feel Good Tracks*. Right, that should do it." She slipped a disc into the CD player and the opening bars to Neil Diamond's *Sweet Caroline* flooded the room.

"Right, come on everyone…hands in the air, that's it." Ava swayed from side to side. "Come on, sway along to the music…that's the way—you too, Jess."

"I think Ava and Harriett have finally gone bonkers," Jess whispered to Lola as she reluctantly raised her arms.

"Oh, and if you're so inclined, you might like to say a little prayer, too," said Ava.

Within minutes, the heavy atmosphere in the room had lifted.

"You know what?" Jess turned to Lola. "I take it all back. Those women are bloomin' marvels. I don't know how they do it."

Forty minutes later, the shrill ring of the phone broke through the music. "I'll get it—you keep swaying." Ava took off her earring and held the receiver to her ear. "Oh, just a minute. Shush, everyone, it's Laura. Yes, yes, oh, thank God! Yes, yes, of course we will. Bye. Fabulous news, everyone—Charlotte's fine." She punched the air. "Nothing to worry about. She'll be home in about half an hour."

As everyone cheered and, as Elvis Presley began to sing about his blue suede shoes, the party really got started.

CHAPTER 8

Aidan Pitt sat on the edge of his desk in his home study, phone between his chin and shoulder, fingers moving swiftly over a calculator keyboard as he brought a conversation with his investment broker to a close.

"Listen, as long as they continue to show growth, don't touch them—if necessary, we'll talk about moving them at a later date. Okay, Maurice, I'll leave them in your capable hands. Keep me in the loop."

He put the phone back in its cradle and opened the door of the study that led into the garden. The sun beat down and he was struck by an uncharacteristic urge to take a break in the middle of the day. *I need to get out. Get away from all this for an hour or so.*

Stress and fear were unfamiliar emotions to Aidan Pitt.

"Stress and fear are for weaklings"*,* he'd been fond of taunting the office minions who had worked for him over the years but now, it unnerved him that the blackmail attempt was causing him a great deal of both.

What he wanted, more than anything, was to track down the blackmailer himself. He smirked as he dreamed about how he would mete out his own, personal brand of justice when he found the person responsible.

However, with time running out and no conceivable way to locate the extortionist, his resolve was beginning to waver.

It went against every one of his principles to relent to the blackmailer's demands but he simply couldn't afford for his secret to become public. It would be the finish of him. He knew he wasn't a reasonable man—he never had been—but, in the light of Nathan's refusal to provide him with protection, he'd begun to wonder if perhaps he should heed the blackmailer's warning and take steps to make amends.

But where to start?

He squinted up at the sky and stretched out his arms, allowing the sunlight to filter through the gaps between his fingers. *I'll think about it when I get back. With Ruby at that cackling women's get-together and Eddie working from home, I'll have plenty of time alone to think about the situation in peace. Yes, I'll figure out what to do later.*

With a considerably lighter step than he'd had for a while, he took the stairs two at a time to change into his workout gear.

Five minutes later, as he sat at his desk writing a note before he left for his run, it occurred to him that something was conspicuous by its absence.

As his eyes searched the room for the missing object he heard the sound of a footstep on the wooden floor behind him.

The first blow to the back of the head rendered him unconscious before he'd even had a chance to turn in his chair.

As he slumped forward, the last thing he saw was the email reminder of the secret he'd carried with him for years.

I know what you did.

ooooooo

"I'll call in and get someone to cover for me. I'll take the rest of the day off." Back at the cottage, Nathan helped Charlotte from the car. "Here, let me carry you inside."

"No! Nathan, I'm fine—really I am. I've got Laura and Jess and Lola and everyone else here. I'll be okay, I promise." Charlotte reached up and planted a kiss on his cheek. "Go on, go back to work and keep us safe from the bad guys."

A fretful Nathan raked a hand through his hair. "Are you absolutely sure? I can easily make arrangements to stay with you."

"Nathan," Laura put her hand on his arm, "stop worrying. She's got wind and she's a little constipated, that's all. If you *really* want an update on either, we'll call you later but, otherwise, relax. Okay?"

"Okay." He gave Charlotte a hug and raised an eyebrow as the sound of raucous laughter and *The Birdie Song* reached his eardrums. "Right, I've been convinced! I'm definitely going." He grinned and settled himself in the car but, just as he was about to drive away, his phone rang.

"Sorry to disturb you, Chief, but you're needed at Aidan Pitt's house as soon as possible." He could just about make out DS Fiona Farrell's voice over the crackly connection.

"What's the problem now?" Nathan did his best to keep his exasperation contained, but Aidan Pitt was trying his patience to the nth degree.

Following their recent meeting, he'd bombarded Nathan with calls, all in an attempt to persuade him to reconsider his decision not to station a number of permanent officers around his home. And all the calls had gone the same way. They'd started with Nathan politely explaining why—without any proof—he wouldn't authorise the manpower, and they'd ended with Aidan

Pitt yelling a stream of profanities before slamming the phone down.

All in all, the fact that Aidan appeared to think he was the most important resident in St. Eves, and that the police force existed simply to be at his personal beck and call, really didn't inspire Nathan to drop everything and rush round to his house. Especially as he had a pile of urgent paperwork on his desk that needed attending to,

"Whatever it is, Fiona, can it wait for an hour or so?"

"Not really, Chief," she replied, the line suddenly clearing.

"Aidan Pitt's been murdered."

ooooooo

"Okay, what do we know so far?"

The gravel drive at the Pitt residence crunched under Nathan's feet as he approached the house.

"We literally came straight here twenty minutes ago after we got the call from the cleaner who found the body, and then I called you," said Fiona. "I've taken a statement from him but he can't tell us much."

"Is there any sign of a break-in? Any forced entry anywhere in the house?"

Fiona shook her head. "No *forced* entry, but the back door in the kitchen was wide open when the cleaner arrived, as was the door from Mr Pitt's study into the garden."

"And where's Mr Pitt?"

"He's in the study. Forensics have just arrived and SOCO got here ten minutes ago."

"Good. Right, let's have a look at him."

Aidan was slouched over his desk, his cheek pushed into the keyboard of his laptop, a pen in his hand and a bloody wound on the back of his head.

"Any weapon been recovered?"

"Not yet, but we're on the case."

Nathan looked around the study. Everything seemed to be in its place with no sign of a struggle.

"It's all pretty tidy in here, Chief," said Fiona. "Wonder if the killer was a stranger who crept up on him, or someone he knew?"

"Hmm, I wonder." Nathan couldn't help but speculate how much of Aidan Pitt's concern for his safety had been based on more than just his intuition.

"D'you know," said one of the SOCO team, "I don't think I've ever seen a private house with so much security. This place would give Fort Knox a run for its money. It's ironic that the deceased had all this stuff to keep him safe and yet, on the day he really needed it, it didn't help him because none of the cameras were switched on.

"According to the cleaner, there'd been some connectivity problems that required the system to be rebooted several times each day. A technician was coming out to look at it tomorrow, apparently. Anyway, we found this—he was evidently writing this note when he was killed. Might be a good starting point in the investigation." He handed Nathan an evidence bag containing a piece of paper with a name written on it.

Jill Travis.

"Mean anything, Chief?" asked Fiona.

"No. Not a thing. So, we'll need to get on it and *make* it mean something."

"And something else you might be interested in." The SOCO team member pressed a key on Aidan's laptop to take it out of sleep mode. "Take a look at this email."

Nathan's expression was grim. "Where did this come from?"

"No idea yet—it's most likely a fake email account—but we'll be checking it out ASAP."

"Make it a priority, will you?" said Nathan. "I want to know, as a matter of urgency, who sent this message. Okay?"

"It sounds serious." Fiona read the message again. "If whoever sent this email is planning to go to the press by the end of the month, it must be about something pretty incriminating, wouldn't you say? He didn't mention anything about being blackmailed to you, did he Chief? When he asked for police protection, I mean?"

"No, not a thing, but I bloody well wish he had." Nathan looked down at Aidan's body. "Right now, though, we need to tell Ruby Pitt. And we need to find the guy who worked for Aidan Pitt. Eric…no, Eddie something or other."

"We don't know where Ruby Pitt is yet, Chief, but we'll start looking."

"Don't bother." Nathan sighed heavily. "I know where she is."

oooooo

"Hello, Eddie? It's DCI Costello. Listen, can you get to *Fisherman's Cottage* on the seafront in St. Eves? It's the white cottage with the hanging baskets, not far from the 'The President' hotel. There aren't any other fisherman's cottages on that stretch of the seafront so you'll know it when you see it. Can you come now? No, I'd rather wait for you to get here before I tell you anything. Okay, thanks."

Nathan and Fiona sat outside the cottage, waiting for Eddie to arrive. The plan was to tell him about Aidan and then get Ruby out of the party and have him be with her for support when they broke the news. It would also give Nathan an opportunity to gauge Eddie's body language—a guilty person's body language gave a lot away.

Without doubt, this was the worst part of the job. Telling someone that a loved one had passed away would never get any easier. And knowing that news of another death—this time, so close to home—would add to Charlotte's stress, only made it harder.

Ten minutes later, Fiona pointed to the tall, rangy figure unfolding itself from the low, white sports car. "Is that him?"

"Yeah, that's him."

"What's going on?" said Eddie, his pleasant face creased with concern. "I called Ruby but she had no idea."

"You called Ruby Pitt?" Nathan and Fiona exchanged concerned looks.

"Yeah, just now. I told her you'd asked me to meet you here, and I knew *she* was here, so I wanted to ask her if she knew what it was all about."

Ruby suddenly appeared at the front door. "What's going on? Why do you need to see Eddie?" She walked down the path towards them.

"Look, this wasn't supposed to happen this way," said Nathan. "I think we should all go down to the station."

"Why? I don't want to go down to the station," said Ruby, becoming agitated.

"Because I'd prefer to go somewhere we can talk."

The opening bars of *Dancing Queen* blared out through the front door, Ava's warbling soprano voice leading everyone in the first verse.

Nathan shook his head. "Somewhere quiet."

"I don't want to go somewhere quiet." Ruby grabbed hold of his arm. "Why can't you tell us here? You're scaring me."

"I really think it would be better if we went somewhere else, Mrs Pitt."

"I'm not moving from this spot until you tell me what's going on." Ruby folded her arms and glared at Nathan and Fiona.

Nathan nodded. "Alright, but not out here. Come with me."

ooooooo

A party welcomed them as they walked through the front door.

A party that came to a stop as soon as Charlotte set eyes on them.

"What is it?" She was on her feet in an instant. "Harriett, turn the music off, please."

Nathan put his hand on her shoulder. "Charlotte, please keep calm, okay. This is nothing for you to worry about. Fiona and I need a word with Ruby and Eddie, that's all, but we'll go through to the garden."

"Eddie, what's going on?" said Penny.

"I don't know but I don't like how I'm feeling," said Eddie, following Nathan outside.

"Can everyone stay inside, please?" said Fiona. "We just need a few minutes."

The colour drained from Ruby's face when Nathan turned to her.

"What is it? What's happened? It's Aidan, isn't it? There's nothing else you'd want to talk to me about."

"I think we should sit down." Nathan sat Ruby on a patio chair and motioned to Eddie to sit beside her.

"I'm so sorry to tell you that your husband was found dead at your home this afternoon."

A confused expression clouded Ruby's face. "What? No, he isn't. He's not dead—he can't be. I saw him this morning before I left. He's at home, he's working. Eddie, what's he talking about?" She reached for his hand but he brushed it away.

"You're wrong, DCI Costello. I saw him this morning, too." Eddie's face had taken on a grey hue. "I called in to pick up some figures I needed for an analysis he wants. You've made a mistake…I'll call him now and you can speak to him." He paced up and down as he dialled Aidan's number with a trembling hand, gasping when he was immediately directed to voicemail.

Aidan Pitt *never* let his calls go to voicemail. He never tired of telling Eddie that every call was a potential money-making opportunity. If a caller couldn't speak to a real person, they'd move on. Opportunity lost.

"Are you sure? Are you sure there's no mistake?" Eddie said, his eyes filling with tears.

"I wish I could tell you there was," said Nathan, "but we're sure. I'm so sorry."

With his head in his hands, Eddie stumbled blindly towards a hysterical Ruby, his knees buckling before he fell to the ground, and they clung to each other and sobbed.

Watching from the kitchen window, Charlotte felt as though she'd been kicked in the stomach as old emotions were brought to the surface.

This party was definitely over.

ooooooo

"Well, yesterday was the stuff nightmares are made of, wouldn't you say?"

As she swept the terrace of the café, Charlotte smashed the broom against the ground with such force, Jess took it from her hands.

"Well, the last hour wasn't great, I'll give you that," said Jess, "but the rest of it was fab."

"But who's going to remember the rest of it after a finale like that? No one, that's who. It'll be known forever more as the baby shower from hell." The frown line between her brows deepened with every word. "Not that I'm not grateful for all the good wishes and the gifts, 'cos I truly am, but after what happened, I can't help feeling that it was a bad omen." She scuffed the toe of her shoe against the ground.

Jess flung down the broom. "Charlotte Costello, you'd better stop thinking that way right now! It was a terrible thing, but to think that something bad's going to happen because of it is just ridiculous, so get that idea out of your head.

Page 129

"And as for worrying about whether people will remember the good bits—for your information, the image of you in that yellow tent-dress will stay with me forever." She giggled and Charlotte's frown disappeared as she recalled the moment, her lips widening in a grin.

"And so will the look on your face when you saw that rocking horse."

Charlotte's smile became even wider and her eyes sparkled. She sniffed and pulled Jess into a hug.

"Y'see," said Jess, returning the hug. "Good stuff always works its magic!"

ooooooo

"Well, it was dreadful." Ava folded the local morning newspaper, its stark headline, *AIDAN PITT DEAD AT 61,* announcing the event of the previous day. "I doubt I'll ever be the same again."

She was holding court at the café, sitting at a table with Harriett, Betty, Leo, and Harry. "And when Nathan told that poor woman and that poor man that Aidan had passed, well, I don't mind telling you, I shed a tear." She patted her eyes with a tissue. "We couldn't *hear* anything from inside, of course, but we could see everything that was going on from the window. I needed a lie-down when I got home. My legs were like jelly."

"I've said it before and I'll say it again," grumbled Harry. "Whenever newcomers upset the balance of the town, you can bet there'll be trouble before long." He poured gravy over his roast beef and tucked a serviette into the front of his shirt. "They're a bloody nuisance."

"Oh, come on, Harry. That's really unfair," said Charlotte, topping up his wine glass from the bottle of Merlot on the table. "The majority of newcomers to St.

Eves are great. And anyway, these people aren't newcomers—they've lived here for years."

"How come I've never seen any of 'em, then?" said Harry, guiding a generously filled fork of meltingly-soft roast beef and crispy roast potato into his mouth.

"Because they live on the other side of town. You don't know *everyone* who lives in St. Eves, you know."

"Do the police have any idea who killed him?" asked Leo, dropping a spoonful of horseradish sauce onto the side of his plate.

"Not yet, but I hope they find out soon," said Charlotte. "The last thing we need is another murderer on the prowl."

oooooooo

Nathan and Fiona Farrell stood on the doorstep of Penny and Owen's house. A ring on the doorbell set off Penny's dogs, and she shushed them to be quiet as she opened the door.

"Morning. Come in, come in. Just ignore the dogs and they won't bother you."

After greeting them at the door and realising that Nathan and Fiona didn't have any treats for them, nor posed any threat, the drooling chocolate Labrador and the dishevelled mongrel retreated to the living room. They each jumped onto a sofa and lay supine and bathed in sunlight, eyes closed, but one ear cocked in the event that someone might mention walkies or sausages.

The dark circles under Penny's eyes told Nathan she hadn't slept well.

"Thank you for agreeing to speak to us, Miss Baker—especially at such a difficult time. Our condolences."

Penny nodded. "I'll be happy to do whatever I can to help. We just can't believe it—first Frankie and now Aidan. By the way, Ruby's upstairs. There was no way she could have gone home last night so I told her she could stay here. She cried so much she exhausted herself, and then she got into such a state she couldn't breathe. We got so scared we called the emergency doctor in the middle of the night and he gave her a sedative which should help her sleep for a few hours, I hope." She wrung her hands. "I think she's going to be staying here for a few days, at least. It's just terrible."

"Are you sure you feel up to answering a few questions?" said Nathan. "We don't have to do this now if you're not."

"No…I mean yes, I'm okay," said Penny. "I'd rather get it over and done with. Come on, come and sit down."

Nathan took his notebook from his pocket. "Would you mind telling me where you were yesterday between quarter-to twelve and when you arrived at the baby shower?"

Penny clasped her hands. "Um, well, Owen, Amy and I were here until about quarter-to twelve. Then Amy and I left to call into town to buy Charlotte a present on the way to the baby shower. Owen stayed here with Zac."

"And can anyone verify that?"

"Well, Karen might be able to," said Penny. "She's the woman over the road who looks after the dogs while we're away. Anyway, Owen was pottering about in the front garden and she was washing her car. He was chatting with her and I waved to her from the front door but I didn't speak to her." She frowned. "Oh, hang on though…that was before midday—around ten o'clock, I think. And Amy was here, too. She's staying here at the moment, so we went to the baby shower together."

Nathan nodded. "Okay, that's great, thank you. And do you have any idea why anyone would have wanted to kill Mr Pitt?"

Penny raised a shoulder. "Well, he wasn't everyone's cup of tea, I'll say that, but I don't know anyone who'd want to kill him."

"What do you mean, 'he wasn't everyone's cup of tea'?"

"Well, he was a bit, you know…a bit pompous," said Penny. "I'm sure he must have rubbed a few people up the wrong way over the years, but enough for someone to want to kill him?" She puffed out a breath. "Who knows? Actually, on reflection, I'm probably not the best person to speak to about Aidan—I didn't know him that well. Owen knew him much better than I did. He'll be back at around half-two. You might be better off speaking to him."

Nathan smiled. "Yes, we'll get to Owen, Miss Baker, but for now you're being very helpful. So, you didn't know Aidan Pitt very well?"

"No, hardly at all. I only know him because he's married to Ruby and Ruby's a friend."

"Ah, well, you see, that's interesting," said Nathan. "Because when we were in London, I saw you meet up with him in Hyde Park. You had a conversation with him. One which appeared to become quite acrimonious from where I was sitting."

Penny opened her mouth and then shut it, colour rising from her neck upwards.

Nathan fixed his eyes on hers. "Would you like to start again, Miss Baker?"

She cursed under her breath. "Okay, I *do* know him—everyone around here knows him. He's Aidan Pitt, for goodness' sake. But I really don't know him very well, and that's the truth."

"I see. So why, considering you don't know him very well, is your number saved in his contacts list?" asked Nathan, just before his phone let out a shrill ring. "Excuse me for a minute, will you, Miss Baker? I should take this." He rose from the couch and moved across the room. "Yes, Ben. You got something?"

"Yes, Chief, we've found some very interesting stuff on Aidan Pitt's laptop," said DS Ben Dillon. "There's a video of a young woman—can't see her face because it's obscured by an umbrella but when forensics enlarged the image, you can see a pretty distinctive tattoo on her chest. It looks fairly new, too, maybe only a few weeks old. It's a heart with the initials AB and FI inside it."

"*What?* Are you sure?"

"Absolutely sure, Chief. We're already working on finding the woman."

"No need. I know who she is. I'll call you when I've finished up here. Good work."

He returned to the couch and turned to Fiona.

"Interesting conversation. Forensics have found some video footage on Aidan Pitt's laptop of a young woman with a very distinctive tattoo on her chest; a heart and some initials, apparently. I think we've found our prime suspect."

Nathan hoped his bluff would prompt Penny to speak, and it paid off.

"Wait a minute," said Penny. "That can't be your suspect? It just can't be."

"And why's that, Miss Baker?"

As she turned an even deeper shade of puce, Penny's shoulders dropped. Leaning her elbows on her knees, she put her head in her hands.

"Because the woman with the tattoo is Amy, and Amy was here all of yesterday morning. Aidan was in a relationship with her for a little while. That's why we had each other's numbers. And I can assure you, that was the *only* reason—if he'd been the last man on earth, I wouldn't have called him for a chat. The man was a sanctimonious pig."

"Can you tell me the reason for your meeting in the park?"

Penny shuffled in her seat. "Because Amy was upset that he'd gone to London and I wanted to ask him to leave her alone. He just wouldn't accept that they were finished even though they'd been apart for months. It made her uncomfortable to have him there—it was like he was spying on her, you know? What with the video camera trained on her apartment and him turning up unexpectedly everywhere she went. I mean, he *never* made the trip to London for the awards. It was so weird that he came along. He hasn't even *got* a tattoo."

"Well, if he and Amy were no longer together, perhaps he went along to keep his wife company," said Nathan. "Not so strange, is it? For a husband to want to be with his wife?"

Penny raised her eyebrows and scoffed. "Not for normal couples, maybe, but Aidan and Ruby were hardly a normal couple."

"I see. And what do you mean by that, exactly?"

She cleared her throat and shuffled some more.

"Are you alright? This line of questioning appears to be making you a little uncomfortable."

"Yes, yes, I'm fine." Penny ran her fingers through her fringe. "Okay, that was a bad choice of words. What I meant is that they're very, er, independent people—Aidan was, especially. Even before he started seeing Amy, his marriage to Ruby was hardly what you'd call conventional. They didn't spend a lot of time together because he was always going off somewhere on business—mainly to check out investment opportunities. He used to take her along with him but she got bored with just sitting around waiting for his meetings to finish so she stopped going. They always got on fine when they *were* together, though."

"Hmm." Nathan scribbled in his notebook. "And have you any idea why someone would have been blackmailing Mr Pitt?"

"What?" Penny's head jerked upwards. "*Blackmailing* him? What on earth was he being blackmailed about?"

Nathan watched her carefully. She might have been lying before but he was sure she knew nothing about the blackmail attempt.

"Okay, just one last question. Do you know anyone by the name of Jill Travis?"

Penny shook her head. "No, I don't. Why? Do you think she's something to do with the blackmail?"

Nathan snapped his notebook shut. "Let's just say she's someone we'd like to speak to. Right, I think that's all for now. Thank you, you've been very helpful."

As he and Fiona stood up to leave, the dogs ran to the front door as they heard a key turn in the lock.

"Hello, darlings. Aunty Amy's bought you some treats…yes she has. Oh, hello."

"Good morning, Miss Baker. How fortuitous," said Nahan. "We were just on our way to your apartment, but you've saved us a trip."

"Oh, really? Why's that?"

"Because, I'd like to ask you some questions. But only if you feel up to it. I know you must have had a terrible shock so, if it's too soon, we can do this later—either here, or somewhere else."

Amy looked at her sister. "Er, well, I suppose so. What do you want to know?"

"Amy, I think it might be better if you went to the station to answer the questions," said Penny. "Or your apartment."

"Why can't I answer them here? I've only just got back and I don't *want* to go out again."

Penny lowered her voice to a whisper. "Because he wants to ask you about Aidan, and Ruby's asleep upstairs. What if she wakes up?"

Amy blushed. "How did he find out about…oh, never mind. Um, okay, just a minute." She gave each dog a dental stick and picked up her keys. "Right. Ready when you are."

ooooooo

"So, what do you want to know?" asked Amy, as they sat around a table in the interview room at the station.

"I'd like to know where you were yesterday between quarter-to twelve and when you arrived at the baby shower."

"Well, I was at Penny's until we left. I can't remember exactly what time it was but it was a little before midday. I like to sleep late at weekends when I can, so I was in bed until around ten-past eleven…and before you ask, I was on my own."

"Okay, thank you. Can you tell me about your relationship with Aidan Pitt?"

"Hmm, I thought you might ask about that. Well, I *first* met him about six months after he and Ruby moved to St. Eves. Owen got to know him at some event or other when he was still working in corporate hospitality, and he organised a clay pigeon shoot so that Aidan and Ruby could meet some people. To be honest, I didn't take much notice of him the first time we met. He was with Ruby and I was with my boyfriend at the time.

"Anyway, fast forward about a year and a half and I bumped into him again at that commerce and music festival that was held in the park. D'you remember it? He was there as a guest of the mayor at the time. He was always looking for something to invest his money in and was involved in supporting local businesses and local people he saw something special in. 'That special quality' he called it.

"Anyway, we were both there on our own and he caught my eye. He was definitely on the lookout for a bit of fun—you can just tell with some people. I was single by then but he was obviously still married. We did a bit of eye-flirting during the afternoon and at the end of the festival, he slipped me his card with his private number on it."

She shrugged. "And that was that. We started seeing each other. He told me I had 'that special quality' and it was great at the beginning. Sneaking around trying to find places to meet so Ruby didn't catch us out was a real thrill. But then he bought me an apartment and everything changed. And not for the better, either." She paused and rubbed her forehead.

"I know that sounds terribly ungrateful but it was too much. He said it would make it easier to get together but I didn't *want* to make it easier—I *liked* the effort of trying to find the time and the place to see each other. It added to the excitement.

"Anyway, it kind of all went flat after he did that. And it made me realise how serious he was, which I definitely wasn't. I just wanted a bit of fun—no strings attached. I kept seeing him because I felt obliged; what with the apartment and the gifts, I didn't feel like I could break it off. But a couple of months ago, I just had to tell him straight.

"He'd started following me and videoing me coming and going from the apartment when I wasn't with him. He was paranoid about security, see, so he had a camera set up outside the building that had a feed straight back to his laptop. Whenever I went out, he'd call me as soon as I got home to ask me where I'd been. It got so creepy, I just couldn't take it anymore."

Amy blew out a breath and tucked her hair behind her ears. "That's why I wanted to talk to you here.

I only really go back to the apartment to pick up stuff these days—I spend as little time there as possible recently. Which is why I'm staying at Penny's. Mind you, I might stay at my place a bit more often now Aidan's not around any more. I know it sounds harsh, but now the initial shock's worn off, I have to say, it's actually quite a relief. That said—and just to be absolutely clear—I didn't kill him."

Nathan and Fiona exchanged a brief glance.

"Do you know who might have wanted to see him dead?" asked Fiona.

Amy shook her heads. "No, I don't. I mean, he told me he'd upset some people over the years but I have no idea who. He must have *really* upset someone for them to have bumped him off, though, don't you think?"

"And what about any blackmail attempts?" said Fiona. "Do you know anything about that?"

Amy frowned. "Blackmail? Sorry, you've lost me."

"Someone was blackmailing Aidan Pitt."

"Really? Oh, I had no idea. What were they blackmailing him about?"

"No idea," said Fiona. "That's what we're trying to find out."

"Well, thank you for sparing us the time on a Sunday morning, Miss Baker," said Nathan. "It was most informative. DS Farrell will see you out. Oh, I'm sorry, two more questions. Does the name Jill Travis mean anything to you?"

Amy shook her head, her long hair swinging at her shoulders. "No. Why? Who is she?"

"Just someone we're interested in speaking to. And my final question… was Mr Pitt jealous of your relationship with Frankie Ingram? I understand you were very close?"

Amy smiled. "Aidan was jealous of my relationships with *everyone*."

As Nathan watched her leave the room, he leaned back and thought about her story. She'd made Aidan Pitt sound like the guilty party.

A minute later, he heard Fiona's returning footsteps and bet himself he couldn't count to three in his head before the onslaught began. He also knew exactly what her reaction to Amy's story would be. He was right on both counts.

"Good grief! I know we're supposed to stay impartial but women like that make my blood boil. How someone could carry on like that with a friend's husband behind her back is beyond me. Well, she *calls* Ruby Pitt a friend but she obviously isn't if she treats her like that. She's a flippin' disgrace!

"And to talk so inappropriately about Aidan Pitt when he only died yesterday! Regardless of how he may have conducted himself, he was still a person. My God, I'd queue up to give that husband-stealing, disrespectful, cold-hearted trollop a piece of my mind, I really would!"

Nathan grimaced. "You know what? I'd be right behind you."

ooooooo

"So, who's your prime suspect?" said Charlotte, who was sitting up in bed, Pippin curled up beside her, when Nathan got home. "Please tell me you've got one."

"No one, at the moment, I'm afraid. Although we now know that Aidan was killed between midday and one o'clock, which is something to go on, at least."

"Well, come and sit down and tell me all about it," said Charlotte. "I've been a bag of nerves, waiting for you to come home."

Nathan told her about his interviews with Penny and Amy, the discovery of the video on Aidan's laptop, and the fact that no one was admitting to knowing anything about the email containing the blackmail attempt.

"If only he'd told me about the email. If only he'd said *something* about it, I would have taken his concerns more seriously, but all he said was that he had a *feeling* something wasn't right—it was intuition, he said. He had nothing to back it up with, though; nothing which made me believe he was under any threat, so I wasn't about to go putting men on security detail on a whim."

Charlotte held his hand. "Don't feel guilty about it. He had the opportunity to tell you about the email but he chose not to. There was no way you could have known what was going on so don't blame yourself. Incidentally, have you spoken to Ruby yet? She might be able to shed some light on it."

"No, not yet. She's been on sedatives so I doubt she'll be in any fit state to talk to us for a day or two. Fiona and I are going to see the first Mrs Pitt on Tuesday afternoon, though."

"What? Aidan's ex-wife?"

"Yep. She obviously kept his name."

"You're hoping she may be able to tell you who this Jill Travis woman is?"

"Amongst other things, yes. And, maybe, give us some clue as to why someone would have been blackmailing Aidan in the first place."

"Well, I'll keep my fingers crossed that she'll be a help, love," said Charlotte, scooping Pippin up in her arms and putting him in his basket.

"I hope to God something is soon," said Nathan before switching off the light.

Chapter 9

"Do you feel up to speaking to us, Mrs Pitt?" asked Ben. "We appreciate you've had a terrible shock, but it's quite possible that something you tell us could help us find whoever killed your husband."

Ruby lay at one end of the corner couch in Penny's living room with Beau, the Labrador, stretched out at the other. She shrugged. "I suppose so, although I'm not sure anything I can tell you will be of any use." She took off her dark glasses and rubbed her puffy, bloodshot eyes. "Oh, I'm so tired, all I want to do is go back to sleep." She yawned and her eyelids drooped.

"Mrs Pitt, are you okay?" Fiona touched her gently on the shoulder.

Ruby blinked and nodded. "Yes, I'm okay. Can we get this over with, please? I want to go back to bed." She picked up a glass of water and shook a pill into her palm from a bottle of prescription medication.

"Of course." Fiona sat down on a nearby chair. "Can you tell me about the last time you saw your husband?"

Ruby tilted her head back to wash down the pill and wiped her hand across her mouth. "It was at home, just before I left for the baby shower. I don't know the exact time but it was around ten-to twelve, I think. I left early because I wanted to call in at the florist on the way to get Charlotte a plant. Aidan was in his study on the phone so I just blew him a kiss and left...that was the last time I saw him and I didn't even say goodbye properly."

She scrunched a handful of hair into a fist. "If only I'd stayed at home. You know, the ironic thing is, I didn't even want to go to the baby shower. I haven't been very good company since Frankie died—I don't think any of us have, really—but Aidan told me to go. He said it would do me good to get out. And, you know what? He was right. I was having a lovely time until DCI Costello turned up."

She simultaneously yawned again and burst into tears, her howls prompting the rest of the household to rush to her aid, and the dogs to rush from the room.

As Penny comforted her, Owen and Zac disappeared into the garden.

"I doubt you'll get any more out of her this evening," said Penny. "Once she starts crying, she can't stop—I expect she'll cry herself to sleep. She's still exhausted and those pills the doctor gave her knock her out."

"Okay, we'll leave it for now."

Before Fiona and Ben had left the room, Ruby was snoring softly.

ooooooo

"The trouble with studio apartments is that everything's in the same room."

Ava, Harriett, and Betty were enjoying afternoon tea at *Charlotte's Plaice*. "Your bed, your TV, your armchairs, your kitchen…I'm not sure I'm keen on that set-up although Derek's trying to talk me round."

"What's wrong with it? A smaller place means that everything's closer to hand." Harriett filled her teacup with Earl Grey before dropping a sugar cube into the delicately perfumed brew.

"I agree with you, Harriett." Betty took a prawn and dill mayonnaise sandwich from the three-tier stand on the table. "It's like the difference between living in a two-storey house and a bungalow. Everything's so much easier since I moved into my retirement bungalow, mainly because I don't have to keep trudging up and down stairs, but also because all the rooms are so much closer together."

"Hmm, well I'm not sure I could ever downsize to that extent." Ava pursed her lips as she stirred her tea, little finger extended at an absurd angle. "I'm used to having space around me."

"Everything alright, ladies?" Charlotte joined them as she took a break from the kitchen.

"Lovely dear, thank you," said Ava. "We were just discussing retirement apartments. Derek's been trying to persuade me that we'd be better off in one but I'm not so sure. I remember my Grandma Doris moving into one. She just couldn't get used to having everything in the same room.

"I shall never forget the first time we went to visit her after she'd moved in—poor dear had almost driven herself to distraction, trying to get BBC1 on the microwave oven. She'd sat down in the kitchen and thought it was the TV. She was terribly confused, bless her."

"I don't know *why* you have this idea stuck in your head that you have to buy a studio apartment," said Harriett. "If you want somewhere bigger, you could get a lovely little place with one or two bedrooms and a separate kitchen that would be perfect for you and Derek. Like Betty's place, for example. You should go and look at one—I'll come with you, if you like. It might even be an option for Leo and me in a couple of years' time. Since we got together we've both been living in separate houses, but it would make much more sense to pool our resources and live somewhere smaller."

"And a lot of them have wonderful social opportunities," said Betty. "You know… a communal room on-site where you can get together and meet the other residents. Not that I've ever bothered with that because I've got you two." She beamed at her two friends.

"Hmm, maybe I'll think about it." Lost in her thoughts Ava stared into space, suddenly realising she was looking straight into the face of a woman who'd just sat down at another table. "Oh, my goodness," she said. "I'm so sorry! You must think me terribly rude. I wasn't staring *at* you—I was staring *past* you, if you know what I mean. I was in a world of my own. My apologies." Ava raised her teacup to the woman, who nodded back at her.

"Don't worry, although I must say I was beginning to wonder if I'd left one of my rollers in. I've done that before now!" The woman laughed.

Sorry, I didn't see you sit down," said Charlotte. "Can I get you something?"

"It's okay, I've just given my order to the other girl. I remembered her from the last time I was here. It's nice to go back to a place and find the same people still there—so many places change hands so quickly these days."

"And it's equally nice when customers like it here enough to come back again," said Charlotte. "We never tire of seeing the same faces over and over. Are you here with friends, or family?"

"Well, I've come to see my son for the day," said the woman. "He brought me to the marina a few years ago when I came to visit and we stopped here for Sunday lunch. We spent a wonderful afternoon together, and this is such a beautiful location—I love marinas.

"Anyway, I got the earlier train so I have a lot of time to kill before he comes to collect me. I had to come back here again—I have such fond memories of this place."

"Well, thank you, that's very nice of you to say." Charlotte cocked her head. "Um, you're probably going to think I'm very nosy but are you Eddie's mum?"

The woman's face lit up. "Yes, I am! How on earth did you know?"

"Because he happened to mention recently that he'd brought his mum here for Sunday lunch a long time ago, and that she liked marinas, and I just made the connection."

"Well, that's very astute of you. I do hope I'll be able to cheer him up. I don't know if you're aware but he's had some terrible news and I've come down to give him a little support. He's dreadfully upset…oh, here's my cappuccino."

"Yes, I know—it *was* terrible news." Charlotte shuddered. "Do wish him well from all of us here, won't you?"

The woman smiled. "Thank you, that's kind. What's your name? I'll tell him you send your regards."

"It's Charlotte."

The woman held out her hand. "Nice to meet you, Charlotte, and I'm Georgina. Georgina Lewis."

ooooooo

"I met Eddie's mum today." Charlotte tied a knot in the bag of tomatoes she'd just weighed and put them in the shopping trolley.

"Did you? Was he with her?" asked Nathan as he examined the label of a bottle of blue wine. "What on earth do they put in wine to make it blue? So, was he?"

"No, but she'd come to visit him for the day. He obviously told her what happened to Aidan and she'd come to give him some motherly love, by the sound of it. She seemed nice."

"Well, perhaps she'll be able to see him a bit more often now that he won't be working 24/7 anymore," said Nathan. "He's going to have a lot of free time on his hands until he gets himself another job."

Charlotte nodded. "You're not kidding. He's worked all the hours of the day and night for so long now, I bet he doesn't know what to do with himself. It can't be easy to make the adjustment. Anyway, I hope his mum will be able to comfort him...he was in such a state after you told him. He took it so badly—he must have been fonder of Aidan than anyone realised."

"Yes, I was surprised at how badly he took the news," said Nathan. "I only wanted him to be there when I told Ruby because I thought he'd be a support to her, but it almost turned out to be the other way round." He shook his head. "You know, you never know what's going on under the surface with some people."

oooooooo

"Pippin, catch!" Charlotte threw a ball across the sand and Pippin raced after it, ears back and tongue hanging out of the side of his mouth.

Nathan had left early to call in at the station before he and Fiona set off to visit Aidan's ex-wife and, rather than turn over and have another hour under the covers after he'd left, Charlotte decided to take Pippin for an early walk.

The sea was rough and she kept a careful eye on the little dog to make sure he didn't pick up anything the surf had washed onto the shore. She was so intent on watching him she didn't see the person running towards her until she were almost at her side.

"Hey! I thought it was you!"

She looked up. "Amy! Hi. What brings you down to this end of town at this time of day?"

Amy removed her headphones. "I always run when I want to clear my head—clear it of all the negative stuff that's going around—and once I started running, I just ended up here. How are you?"

"Oh, okay. Still trying to forget about everything that's happened recently but, apart from that, I'm fine. You?"

"Well, we're all just trying to get on with stuff," said Amy. "Sometimes I'm okay and sometimes I can't stop crying. I felt *really* low when I woke up this morning—thinking about Frankie, you know?"

They walked along the beach, a gust of wind blowing sand in their faces every now and then.

"How's Ruby?"

"Hmmm, not good. Now I know how worried Penny must have been about me right after Frankie died. It's like she's turned into a zombie. All she does is sleep, and when she wakes up she takes another sleeping pill, and so it goes on. She doesn't know it, but we've made an appointment for her to see the doctor tomorrow morning. She can't carry on the way she is. She won't be fit for Frankie's memorial if she does, and I know she really wants to be there. Will you be coming, do you think?"

They stopped to sit on the wall that ran the length of the seafront.

"I think so but I'll confirm nearer the time. Nathan won't be, I know that for sure, but I'll confirm with you by Thursday. Is that okay?"

"That'll be fine. Give either Penny or me a call. Right, I'd better head back." Amy took off her tracksuit jacket. "Phew, that's better. Funny how you get warmer when you stop running, instead of cooling down, isn't it?"

Tying the jacket around her waist, she settled the scooped neckline of the t-shirt she was wearing underneath.

Charlotte did a double-take. She pointed. "Your tattoo."

The tattoo on Amy's chest was clearly visible. Two cherubs either side of a heart emblazoned with a pair of initials.

Amy frowned. "Yes, what about it?"

"I thought they were Frankie's initials."

"What? Why on earth would you think that?"

"Because I've never seen the whole thing," said Charlotte. "I've only ever seen the top of it and I assumed it said AB and FI."

"Good grief, no!" said Amy. "Frankie was my best friend in the world but he was like a brother, God bless him. I can't *believe* you thought that! I'll admit, I *was* keeping it covered up for a little while because…er, oh, never mind. It doesn't matter who sees it now."

"So, now that I can see the whole thing," said Charlotte, "and I can see that the initials are EL and not FI, would I be right in thinking that EL is…"

"Eddie," said Amy. "EL is Eddie Lewis."

ooooooo

"Good afternoon, Mrs Pitt. I'm Detective Chief Inspector Nathan Costello and this is DS Fiona Farrell. I spoke with you yesterday. I'm sorry we're a little late."

Nathan and Fiona stood at the front door of the smart white house with the red tiled roof, where a tall, homely woman with shoulder-length mousy hair, pale blue eyes and rosy cheeks smiled warmly in welcome.

"Oh, don't worry, no harm done, dear. You want to talk about Aidan, don't you? Come in, please. You've come so far—did you drive or take the train?"

"We drove, although, on reflection, the train would probably have been a better idea," said Nathan. "Less traffic."

"Oh dear, you poor things. It's a three-hour drive, isn't it? The traffic must have made it so much longer. You must be terribly thirsty."

She took them into a cosy room, dominated by two arm chairs with large throws covering them.

"Please, sit down—and take the arm chairs. The throws cover the cat hair. Not that I'm bothered by it—I don't possess an item of clothing that isn't covered in the stuff—but I don't expect you want it all over you, do you? I'll sit on the couch. Now, I've just made a pot of tea. Would you like a cup?"

Hamburgers, Homicide and a Honeymoon

Tea and biscuits on the table, Nathan began his questioning.

"First of all, Mrs Pitt, I'd like to offer our condolences."

She waved his sympathy away. "No condolences necessary. I'm completely indifferent to his demise."

"I see. Well, there are two reasons for our visit."

She eyed Nathan curiously. "Tell me."

"One, to ask if you know anything about a blackmail attempt against your ex-husband and, two, to ask if the name Jill Travis means anything to you."

Nathan noticed that the hand holding the teacup shook a little at the mention of Jill Travis. *At last, we could be on to something here.*

Mrs Pitt put down her cup. "Yes, I know who Jill Travis is but I have no idea where she is now, or even if she's still alive."

"And can you tell me who she is?"

"I can, but it'll make more sense if I tell you the whole story—do you have a while?"

"We've got all the time in the world," said Nathan."

"Okay, but I should warn you that there's no happy ending to this story, and none for me, either. But I'll accept the punishment for my sins—I've been waiting a long time for the police to come knocking on my door…"

ooooooo

"Years ago, when Aidan first started out in the property business, the construction company was very small. He was always one to bend the rules…didn't like others bending them, mind, but it was okay for him to do it. Anyway, he bribed a planning official to approve his plans to build on protected land.

"He built a number of luxury apartment blocks, all of which were snapped up, off-plan, for a small fortune. The deal made him a millionaire overnight, which, in those days, was no mean feat, I can tell you. Whatever anyone may have said about Aidan, he had an eye for a business like you wouldn't believe.

"Anyway, a few years later, Aidan found out that the planning official was intending to confess his part in the deal and threatening to bring the scandal to light."

Mrs Pitt dabbed at her forehead with the back of her hand.

"That planning official was David Travis, and I know about all of this because his wife, Jill, told me everything. Out of some misguided loyalty to Aidan, I've kept it to myself for all these years, for reasons which will become clear.

"When Aidan discovered the deal might be in danger of being revealed, he arranged to meet David so they could come to some agreement to keep the matter between themselves. Knowing Aidan as I did, I knew he would have been furious at the prospect of serving a possible prison sentence because some pen-pusher, as he called them, wanted to clear his guilty conscience.

"One evening, he told me he had a meeting. I remember it well, because it was completely out of the blue at nine o'clock. I'd had my suspicions about his fidelity for months, you see."

"He was unfaithful?" said Fiona.

Mrs Pitt's eyebrows shot up. "Oh yes, Aidan liked the women, alright, so when the opportunity arose to catch him with his pants down, I didn't think twice about taking it. As soon as he left the house that evening, I jumped in my car and followed him.

"I thought he was on his way to a hotel, so you can imagine my surprise when he pulled onto an industrial estate—hardly the place to meet a fancy woman. He parked the car and walked up an alleyway that led to an unused car park, and I parked in an unlit spot and set off behind him to see what he was up to. I was careful to keep well in the shadows—the last thing I wanted was for him to catch sight of me and call off his meeting.

"I watched him from the alleyway and, after a minute or two, a man turned up. I'd never seen him before but I remember he looked middle-aged, and was wearing a light-coloured suit. I didn't find out until later that the man was David Travis.

"They talked for around ten minutes and, just as I was debating whether to stay or leave, Aidan punched him. It all happened so quickly, I almost missed it. David fell backwards and hit his head on a kerbstone. I thought Aidan would help him but he just looked at him once and then turned and walked away.

"I ran back to my car as fast as I could and crouched down in the seat. I heard Aidan get in his car and drive away, but I stayed like that for a long time, wondering what to do. In the end, I drove to a phone box and called 999 to report a man with head injuries, and told them to send an ambulance to where Aidan had left him. I made sure it was a quick call and I talked through my handkerchief to muffle my voice. It's amazing the things you pick up from watching murder mysteries on TV, you know."

She smiled weakly and took another sip of her tea.

"Then I drove home. Aidan's car wasn't in the drive, and I guessed that he'd most likely gone somewhere to provide himself with an alibi should he need one—the local pub, as it turned out.

"I poured a large vodka and tonic and took it into the living room. When Aidan got home an hour later, he sat beside me on the couch and told me he needed help. He'd got into a bit of trouble, he said. Nothing serious, but if anyone was to ask where he'd been that evening, I was to say he'd been home with me all night, apart from when he'd gone to the pub for an hour. I asked him what kind of trouble he was in and he told me it was nothing for me to worry about.

"The next morning, the local news reported that a David Travis had been found with a serious head injury—the victim of a suspected robbery, they said. Two days later, a report came through that he'd died of his injuries.

"I watched Aidan during that news bulletin. He barely glanced at the TV before carrying on with the crossword puzzle in the morning paper. Not one flicker of emotion. That was when I knew the man I'd married was a monster." Her voice quavered. "Isn't it silly? Even now, it still gets to me."

"We can stop for a while, if you like? Carry on in an hour or so." Nathan hadn't been expecting anything like this. Accusations, confessions, and a story he could never have dreamed of. He would stay for as long as she wanted to keep talking.

"No, it's okay. Now I've started, it feels good to get it off my chest after so long. But thank you for offering." She smiled and patted Nathan's hand.

"Now, where was I? Oh, yes…well, because Aidan's construction company had such close ties with the planning office, it was taken for granted that he would attend David's funeral but on the day, he made an excuse not to go. I was furious with him but he wouldn't change his mind so I went on his behalf. After the service, Jill Travis came over and spoke to me.

"She told me her husband had confessed to her about taking a bribe from Aidan. Apparently, he just couldn't live with the guilt and was considering owning up to what he'd done to the police. She told me that Aidan had contacted David and asked to meet with him. Apparently, David was sure he was going to offer him money to keep his mouth shut but he wouldn't have taken it. Anyway, they planned to meet on the night David died.

"Jill asked me if I knew what really happened. She never believed he was the victim of a robbery, you see. She believed Aidan had something to do with his death, and she told the police, but when they'd contacted him, he denied all knowledge of a meeting with David. Even though she was convinced he was involved, she couldn't prove it.

"I told her I felt for her, but she was mistaken. I told her Aidan had been at home with me that night…apart from the one hour he'd spent at the pub. Misguided loyalty, like I told you. I never spoke to or saw Jill Travis again." Mrs Pitt dabbed at her forehead and sighed.

"You know, not a day goes by that I wish I'd had the courage to report Aidan to the police, but I was too scared. I'd seen him sweet-talk his way out of so many situations in the past, I honestly thought he'd be able to persuade the police he'd done nothing wrong and they'd let him go. And if he ever found out that I'd turned him in, I know he'd have come after me. So I said nothing.

"Anyway, after six months of living a lie, pretending that everything between us was okay, I woke up one morning to find a note on the kitchen table that said, 'Sorry, this isn't working. My solicitor will be in touch.' He'd left me. Just like that."

She took a tissue from the pack Fiona passed her and wiped it across her face.

"It was such a shock, I didn't know whether to laugh or cry. But I knew I'd be better off without him. That's why I never went after him for spousal support—I wanted to prove to myself I could do okay without him. And I have."

"You never considered remarrying?" asked Fiona.

"No, never wanted to. But I've never been lonely—not once," she said, with a smile. "You see, I got my life back the day he left, like I could never have imagined."

"Well, that's one good thing to come of this whole sorry situation, I suppose," said Fiona.

Mrs Pitt nodded and rose from the couch. "Well, detectives, I think I've answered your question about Jill Travis more than adequately but, regarding who could have been blackmailing Aidan, that, I'm afraid, I can't help you with. Now, if I could ask a small favour?"

ooooooo

Talking to Nathan and Fiona had convinced Mrs Pitt to finally make a formal statement to the police force who'd investigated the death of David Travis all those years ago.

"Would you mind taking me to the station, please?" she asked. "I think it's time for me to tell the truth at last."

As they waited in the station foyer, Fiona turned to Nathan. "Well, I wasn't expecting to learn all that by coming here today, were you, Chief?"

Nathan shook his head. "I suppose Jill Travis must be the person Aidan Pitt was going to make amends with for hurting so deeply? Why else would her name have been in a note he was writing before he was killed?"

"I'd say that's likely," said Fiona. "It's just a shame that he'll never be able to make amends now. I wonder if Ruby Pitt knows about his past?"

"I'd be surprised if Aidan told her," said Nathan. "It's not the sort of thing you'd confess to your new wife, I wouldn't think. Ah, here comes our information."

An officer approached, shaking his head. "Sorry, DCI Costello, our records show that Jill Travis died six years ago and her only child passed away a couple of months ago. No other relatives as far as I can see."

"Damn it. Okay, thanks." Nathan's plan to pay a visit to Jill Travis, if she still lived in the area, had just come to a grinding halt.

"What now, Chief? Back to St. Eves?"

"Yep, back to St. Eves."

oooooo

"Hi. I come bearing wine for me, apple juice for you, and a treat for Pippin."

Jess kissed Charlotte on the cheek and handed her two bottles. "Yes, yes, I've got something for you, too," she said to the little dog, who was sitting up, ears alert and tail brushing back and forth across the floor. She threw him a chicken jerky strip and he trotted off with it, disappearing behind the couch. "Mmmm, what's cooking?"

"Chicken casserole and baked potatoes, with optional garlic butter and melted cheese. Optional for you, that is, not me. I'm having it all…with some gherkins and pickled onions on the side. And help yourself to tortilla chips and guacamole."

As Charlotte opened both bottles and they sat down at the kitchen table, Jess picked up *The Great Big Book of Baby Names* from the counter.

"Blimey! 50,000 names! Decided on anything yet? Or is it a secret?"

"Well, it's not a secret because we haven't made our minds up yet. We'd both like to see the baby before we choose a name for it, though. Otherwise we could pick something and it won't suit it. Do you know what I mean?"

"What, you mean you could choose a name like Bert and then it wouldn't be suitable because it'd be a girl?" Jess winked and opened the bag of tortilla chips.

"Ha-ha, very funny," said Charlotte, and poked out her tongue. "Don't stuff your face with those, will you, or you won't be able to eat your dinner, and it's chicken casserole with dumplings."

Jess's eyes widened. "Dumplings? I *love* dumplings!"

"I know you do," said Charlotte, with a grin. "That's why we're having them. Anyway, I feel like we haven't had an evening together in ages. We used to get together all the time."

"Ah, yes, those were the days…I remember them well." Jess gazed reminiscently into space. "The days when we were young, footloose, and fancy free—before we were grown-ups and you got tied to the old ball and chain…where is he, by the way?" She dipped a chip into a guacamole mini-mountain.

Charlotte giggled. "You're such an idiot…and the 'old ball and chain' is on his way back from a meeting, but he's going back to the station first so you might not see him before you leave."

"So, how're you coping with all the madness?" said Jess, scooping up more guacamole. You'd better promise me you won't let everything that's going on stress you out—I know what you're like at the best of times."

"Well, I'm trying not to get stressed, but it's not easy to relax when you know there's a murderer on the prowl. I mean, you must feel a little anxious, too, surely?" Charlotte pushed her fist into the small of her back, the all-too-familiar twinge making her wince.

Jess shrugged. "A little, I suppose, but I just try not to think about it." She crunched into another overloaded chip and wiped the corners of her mouth with her little finger.

"Well, I wish it was all over and done with," said Charlotte. "Murderers behind bars and life back to normal. I keep going over and over what happened in

London, trying to work out if there was any link between Frankie's death and Aidan's death."

Jess rolled her eyes. "Why are *you* trying to work *anything* out? That's what the police are doing. Leave it up to them."

"I know, I know, I should, but I've got this niggling feeling that I'm missing something. Like I've forgotten something that's really important, or there's something really obvious staring me in the face and I haven't seen it. I can't shake it and it's driving me mad."

"Okay then." Jess topped up her wine glass and sat back in the chair. "Tell *me* everything that happened. Maybe you can't see it because you're too close to it. Perhaps something will jump out at me."

"I've already told you everything—you know as much as I do." Charlotte scratched her head. "But basically, Frankie and Amy were rushing to get to the hot tub, he jumped in first, got electrocuted, and everyone was devastated. We all came home, someone clunked Aidan over the head, and no one is any the wiser about why either of them is dead. That's all there is to tell, really." She took the casserole out of the oven and gave it a stir before adding four dumplings to simmer in the gravy for half an hour. "Actually, there *is* one more thing I thought might be relevant but, since Aidan died, my theory's gone out the window."

"And what theory is that?"

"Well, just before we left the house in London after Frankie's death, I could have sworn Aidan had a smug look on his face. Sort of self-satisfied. It made me wonder if he was involved in some way, but now…oh, I don't know what to think."

"But you still think the deaths are connected?"

Charlotte nodded. "I do. I mean, two deaths in as many weeks of people in the same circle of friends—it's just too much of a coincidence, don't you think? The only thing is I can't believe that any of them would kill anyone. I don't know them very well but none of them strike me as murderers. I don't know—maybe I'm overthinking things, but I can't get rid of the feeling that I'm missing something that should be obvious."

"Well, I'm sure the police will work it out," said Jess, squeezing Charlotte's hand. "Nathan, Ben, Fiona, and everyone else are working all hours to get to the bottom of it. Please don't make yourself anxious by taking on stuff that you have absolutely no control over."

As Charlotte served up dinner, it occurred to her that the advice both Nathan and Jess had given her was almost identical.

She guessed they'd been discussing how to reassure her, given her disposition to overreact to bad news, and she smiled as it dawned on her—she was so lucky to have them.

As she spooned chicken casserole onto Jess's plate, she added an extra dumpling.

CHAPTER 10

"You look shattered," said Charlotte.

"I feel shattered. We should have taken the train. There was traffic almost all the way there and all the way back." Nathan hugged her as Pippin ran in circles around their feet.

"Dinner's all ready. I'll dish up now, if you're hungry."

"I'm starving, thanks." He took a bottle of water from the door of the fridge. "How was your day…you been okay? Did Jess come round?"

"Yes, everything's fine and yes, she did. I've got something to tell you, though. Come and sit down. You're never going to believe it."

"I'm all ears." Nathan speared a chunk of chicken with the tip of his knife and popped it into his mouth. "Mmm, this is good."

"So, this morning I was out with Pip on the beach, and you'll never guess who I bumped into?"

"You're right, I'll never guess," said Nathan, focusing on his dinner plate.

"Amy Baker. She was out on a run."

"Really? That's a good distance. She must be pretty fit."

"Anyway, when she took off her tracksuit jacket, I saw her tattoo. The one here." Charlotte tapped a finger on her chest.

Nathan glanced up. "And? What about it?"

"It doesn't say AB and FI."

"Yes, it does. I've seen it on that video."

"No, Nathan, it doesn't. We've only ever seen the top of it and *assumed* that's what it said. It actually says AB and EL."

Nathan put down his knife and fork. "So when you see the whole thing, top and bottom, it says EL, not FI?"

Charlotte nodded. "Eddie Lewis."

"Bloody hell! That answers a lot of questions. I bet that's why Amy wanted a swimsuit that covered it up at the barbecue, because she didn't want Aidan to see it."

"Gosh, yes!" said Charlotte. "Because he had no idea that she and Eddie were seeing each other. Oh my goodness, can you imagine? He probably would have gone ballistic."

"Well, well, well, talk about a dark horse. Knowing what I know now about Aidan Pitt, I'd say that Eddie was playing a very dangerous game. Thank God Aidan never found out about it, or we might have had three dead bodies on our hands instead of two."

"Dangerous game? What d'you mean?"

Nathan told Charlotte about his meeting with Aidan's ex-wife. About how Aidan had extinguished the life of someone who'd got in his way without a second thought. And how he'd left her all those years ago without a word of warning.

"That's awful," said Charlotte, her eyebrows dipped in a frown. "I don't like to speak ill of the dead, but it sounds like she was better off without him. And Ruby, too. What's she like, out of interest? His ex, I mean. Is she anything like Ruby? I imagine her to be a very glamorous older woman."

Nathan shook his head. "Definitely not. Pleasant-looking, yes. Glamorous, no. Georgina Pitt is nothing like Ruby."

"Georgina? Really? That's a coincidence," said Charlotte. "Eddie's mum is called Georgina, too. But Georgina Lewis, obviously."

There was a moment of silence as the implications of Charlotte's words sank in.

Nathan put down his knife and fork. "Eddie's mum…what does she look like?"

"Um, mousy hair, down to here," Charlotte touched her shoulder, "blue eyes, kind face, rosy cheeks. Not as tall as Eddie, but tall."

Nathan shook his head. "Lewis must be her maiden name. I'll bet money on it…Eddie is Aidan Pitt's son."

ooooooo

"I can't take all this in," said Charlotte. "Georgina Lewis and Georgina Pitt are the same person? And she never said anything to you about having a son when you went to see her this afternoon?"

"Not a thing," said Nathan.

"I wonder if it was Eddie who killed Aidan?" said Charlotte. And then, quietly, "I'm pretty sure he knows that Aidan was his dad."

"Why do you think so?"

"Because his reaction to the news of Aidan's death was exactly how I reacted when the police told me about my mum and dad. The way his legs gave way, and the grief—it was so intense. Watching you tell him made me feel physically sick because it brought it all back to me."

Nathan pulled her onto his lap. "Oh, Charlotte, I'm so sorry. That never even occurred to me. You should have said something."

"What good would it have done? Anyway, it doesn't matter—I'm just telling you why I think I'm right."

They sat in silence, going over the permutations of the situation until Charlotte gripped Nathan's hand.

"That's why Eddie didn't want to give a DNA sample—not because he was afraid it would identify him as the person who tampered with the hot tub, like we originally thought—but because it would identify him as Aidan's son and he didn't want anyone to know."

Nathan planted a kiss on her lips. "Do you know what, Mrs Costello?"

"What?" said Charlotte, sliding her arms around his neck.

"If you carry on like this, you'll make Sergeant in no time."

ooooooo

"Eddie. It's DCI Costello and DS Dillon. Will you open the door, please?"

The sound of shuffling preceded Eddie's gaunt, unshaven face peering around the edge of the open door.

"I'm sorry, can this wait? I'm really not in the mood to speak to you just now."

"No, Eddie, it can't," said Nathan. "We've delayed questioning you because you've been too upset to speak to us but we can't put it off any longer. Can we come in, please? Or you can come down to the station, if you'd prefer?"

With a sigh of resignation, Eddie moved back to let them in. "Living room's the second on the right." He slumped down into an old leather chair and ran a hand across his face. "So what d'you want to talk to me about that's so urgent?"

"Did you murder Aidan Pitt?" Nathan's first question caught him off guard.

"What? No. God, no, I swear I didn't. I couldn't—" Eddie put a thumb in his mouth and began to chew the nail. "You don't understand."

"I think I do," said Nathan. "Aidan Pitt was your father, wasn't he?"

The look on Eddie's face alone confirmed the answer to the question.

"How do you know? How did you find out?" He put his fingers through his hair and shook his head. "Oh God! Did my mum tell you? I really don't want to talk about it."

Nathan sat down opposite him, his voice kind. "No, your mum didn't tell us but you're going to have to sooner or later—why don't you just tell us now?"

Eddie sniffed. "I wish I'd told him now that I was his son...I *should* have told him and now it's too late. I was going to wait until the end of the month to tell him—when he was frantic with worry that his blackmailer was about to spill his dirty little secret to the press, but—"

Nathan interrupted. "His blackmailer? You know about that?" The realisation dawned. "It was *you* who was blackmailing him? *You* sent the email?"

Eddie looked terrified. "You didn't know? I thought that's why you were here." He punched the arm of the chair. "Damn it! I should have kept my mouth shut!"

"Eddie, you need to help me understand all this because I need to know." Nathan took off his jacket and rolled up his sleeves. "I have a feeling we're going to be here for a while. Now, please. Tell me everything."

Eddie bit his bottom lip and blew out a deep sigh.

"My mum was pregnant with me when my dad left. She didn't tell him because she didn't want him to know anything about me. She wanted to keep me away from him. He never even knew I existed.

"Mum kept a diary about everything my dad did. She said she wrote it for cathartic reasons—to help ease her conscience. That diary became a record of every terrible thing he had ever done, from the way he treated her like dirt to the part he played in the death of that guy, David Travis.

"When I was fourteen, I found the diary when I was looking for cigarettes in her room—she used to hide them from me, y'see. Anyway, after I'd read it, I asked her to tell me everything about him—I wanted to know it all. Because she'd never bad-mouthed him to me, I had no idea what he was really like. I just assumed he was an ordinary guy who left home one day. Kids don't analyse information so much when they're young.

"She told me everything about him. He was pretty successful by then but I didn't want to find him or anything like that, I just wanted to know about my dad. I thought it'd make me feel good, but the older I got, the angrier I got. D'you know, he left my mum without a penny? She didn't want anything from him so she never asked him for money, but you'd have thought he'd have the decency to offer her something." He smashed his fist down on the arm of the chair again.

"I knew I had to get back at him for what he'd done and I knew the best way to do that was to get close to him. So I read everything I could. He was doing well for himself so it wasn't hard to find articles about him in the business sections of the newspapers. I followed his every move and spent every spare minute learning about him. I studied hard to get good qualifications and, when I was ready, I contacted him to ask him to keep me in mind if he ever needed a personal assistant.

"I made sure the letter was really smarmy and complimentary—I told him I'd be honoured to work for him, blah, blah, blah. I knew how vain he was and Mum had told me that stroking his ego was the way to get his attention. She never thought I'd get the job but I knew I would—because I knew what made him tick. Flattery. I flattered him until he felt so good he couldn't *not* give me the assistant's job.

"Anyway, it worked because he contacted me personally and told me to come for an interview. My surname is Lewis, which is my mum's maiden name, but it's a common enough name not to have rung any alarm bells with him. So I went for the interview and he offered me the job on the spot. That was five years ago. It was just a matter of time before I put my plan to ruin him into place."

"But why did you wait so long? Why didn't you blackmail him before? Why wait all these years?" asked Nathan.

"Because I wanted to lull him into a false sense of security. I wanted him to get to know me and trust me—I wanted to be the last person on earth he'd suspect of trying to bring him down. And it was working. He didn't suspect me for a minute. He was paying me overtime to find out who was sending the emails.

"The thing is, as much as I wanted to hate him, over the years I grew to respect him. He would get everything and anything he wanted. He was so powerful, I began to feel proud that he was my dad.

"All the feelings I'd had about wanting to deprive him of knowing he had a son, changed to wanting to tell him he had one. So I decided to teach him a lesson. I was going to make him *think* his dirty little secrets were going to be made public at the end of the month, just to make him sweat, and then I was going to tell him all about me and that the blackmail attempt had just been my way of getting back at him."

"And Amy? Did she know about the blackmail attempt?"

Eddie looked surprised. "So you know about me and Amy?" He rubbed his hand over his stubbled chin. "No, she didn't know anything about it, I swear she didn't. No one knew anything about it apart from mum and me."

He exhaled a deep sigh. "You know, when it became obvious how much Aidan loved Amy, I knew I was going to try to steal her away from him—just because I knew how much it would hurt him.

"The thing is I didn't expect to like her, let alone fall in love with her. Taking Amy away from him on my terms was one thing, but falling in love with the woman *he* loved was another thing altogether. He would have killed me if he'd found out—and possibly Amy, too.

Even *after* she left him he was so possessive—it's ironic that his possessiveness was one of the reasons she left him in the first place."

"Tell me about the trip to London," said Nathan.

"Ah, yeah, London. Well, that was supposed to be just the gang. Amy and me had been looking forward to it for ages—it was our first real time away together and we were going to tell everyone about us—but all of a sudden, Aidan decided to come along, and Amy and me had to pretend we were just friends."

He flung himself back on the chair. "You know, he wanted to go to London to kill Frankie—can you believe it? Or, should I say, he wanted *me* to go to London to kill Frankie—'make it look like an accident', he said."

Nathan's brow shot up. "And what did you say?"

"I told him not to be so ridiculous, of course," said Eddie. "He was convinced that Frankie and Amy were having a thing because he'd seen her tattoo on the CCTV and he thought it said AB & FI. I'll never forget the day he showed me that video—I thought he'd rumbled us. Thank God he never knew what the tattoo really said. That's why Amy had to stay covered up in London."

"Anyway, when Aidan realised I wanted no part of murdering Frankie, he backed down. He had no intention of doing the deed himself—not when there were so many of us staying at the house and he could so easily have been found out—so, instead, he just hung around, watching Amy's every move. When Frankie ended up dead, we were all devastated, but he was over the moon."

"But do you think he killed him?" asked Nathan.

"No, I don't. But you remember me telling you how he always got what he wanted? Well, that was Aidan for you—everything always seemed to go his way. Eddie wrung his clammy hands. "Look, I never meant for anyone to get hurt. I might have wanted to a long time ago, but I swear I didn't kill anyone. Not Frankie or Aidan.

"If you're looking for a murderer, you're not going to find one here."

CHAPTER 11

"Yooohooo, only me!"

"We're in here, Ava." Jess looked over the top of the swing door of the kitchen.

"Hello, dears. I wanted to give you this book, Charlotte. I just found it in the charity shop in town."

"Oh, thank you, Ava." Charlotte went out into the café. "You shouldn't have." She took the book, her smile fading as she read the title.

"What's it called?" said Jess.

Charlotte forced the smile back on her face. "It's called, *Fifty Ways Not to Be a Pain in the Butt When You're Expecting.*"

"I assume it's an American book," said Ava, looking very pleased with herself. "Otherwise it would say bottom, not butt. No matter, dear, I'm sure the advice translates to all nationalities."

Jess threw her head back and roared with laughter. "Ava, you're an absolute gem! I don't know what we'd do without you but I'm pretty sure we wouldn't laugh half as much as we do now!"

As Charlotte saw the funny side, she started to giggle. "Thank you, Ava. I'm sure it'll be very interesting." She gave her old friend a hug and thought for the millionth time how fortunate she was to have her in her life. No matter how inappropriate her comments or her gifts, her heart was always in the right place and her intentions were always good. Jess was right. Ava was an absolute gem.

"So, are you staying for a coffee or is this just a flying visit?"

"I'm meeting Harriett at three and we've got some friends joining us." Ava looked at her watch. "I don't think you've ever met Cindy and Brenda, have you? They're the founding members of 'The Pittettes'—you know, the Aidan Pitt appreciation society. As you can imagine, they've been distraught following recent events, so Harriett and I thought we'd invite them out, you know, to see if we can lift their spirits a little.

"Anyway, dears, I'll have a cup of tea, today, I think. Just a little milk, please, Jess. And I'll go and grab that table in the shade before someone else nabs it. It's terribly hot out there this afternoon and I don't want my makeup to melt."

ooooooo

"The one in the green jumpsuit keeps calling me Tess. I keep correcting her but she keeps doing it," Jess whispered to Charlotte. "And they're very intense, aren't they?"

"You can say that again. Especially the one with the perm and the pearls. Leo was right, they really do have an encyclopaedic knowledge of Aidan Pitt. Dates, times, places, what happened and when—I don't know how they remember it all."

Charlotte had just spent fifteen minutes trying to politely excuse herself from the company of Brenda Tatum, who, following a visit to the ladies room, had insisted on sharing her memories of Aidan throughout the years. Charlotte wondered how popular he would have been if 'The Pittettes' had known about his secret past.

"Charlotte! Jess! Oh, you must come and look at these photos. They're priceless!" Ava beckoned them from the table outside. "Come and see!"

Charlotte and Jess exchanged a glance.

"Well, I can't go out, I've got prep in the kitchen to get on with," said Charlotte.

"And I can't go because I've got...er, I've got...customers to serve! Yippee! I win!" Jess picked up her tray and skipped out to tend to a family of four who had just settled themselves at a table.

Charlotte sighed. She'd never been particularly interested in Aidan Pitt, but recent revelations had made her even less so. Nevertheless, a customer was a customer, whoever they might be.

Putting the smile back on her face, she called out, "Coming, Ava!"

ooooooo

"So the neighbour's sticking to her story?" said Nathan.

The investigations into Frankie Ingram's murder in London, and Aidan Pitt's in St Eves, had become so intertwined, Nathan hoped Toby Carter might have some information that would shed new light on Aidan's death.

"Not only is the old dear sticking to her story but she's got a date now," said Toby. "Until yesterday, all she could tell us was that she was sure she saw someone at the Baker house in March. But yesterday, she called to let me know it was the third weekend in March."

"And you think that's reliable information?" asked Nathan.

"Well, between you and me, she's too much of a busybody for my liking, but those are the people who very often give the most reliable info; because they've always got their noses into everything, they don't miss much, see?"

"So why has she only just remembered about it being the third weekend in March?"

"Because she had some dental work done on the Friday of that weekend. She said she didn't immediately make the connection between the couple arriving at the house being on the same date she had her teeth fixed, because the anaesthetic had made her drowsy and she spent most of the weekend in bed. Her daughter had dropped her home from the dentist that evening at around six-thirty and that's when she saw the couple arriving at the house but, because it was dark, and she was still groggy, she didn't notice anything other than it was two people.

"It wasn't until the Sunday afternoon that she caught sight of the couple from an upstairs window, albeit from a distance but, because they were wrapped up so well against the cold, she couldn't see much. She's adamant, though, that she saw some strands of blonde hair coming out from under the woman's hat. She said the woman was wearing a black coat and a black hat, so the blonde hair was very noticeable."

"Have you told the Baker sisters?" asked Nathan.

"Yeah, I just spoke to Penny and she said she and her sister took the baby to visit their parents who were on holiday in France that weekend, and her partner, Owen, went clay pigeon shooting from Friday until Sunday afternoon with Aidan Pitt and Eddie Lewis. She's adamant that no one was at the house that weekend and our witness is mistaken."

"I see. I take it you've not had the DNA results back yet?"

"No, but it should be any day now," said Toby. "I'll let you know when I have any news. So, how are things going with the Aidan Pitt case?"

"Well, there have been a few developments but nothing that points to the identity of the killer," said Nathan. "It's frustrating, that's for sure."

"Tell me about it." Toby Carter chuckled. "Well, I'd better be going, places to go, people to see...you know how it is."

"Yeah, I do. Okay, keep in touch and I'll do likewise. Speak to you soon."

Nathan had a hunch. He tried to ignore it but it bothered him until he couldn't ignore it any longer.

Picking up his keys, he called out to Amanda. "I'll be back in an hour or so. Call me with anything urgent."

The hunch didn't directly concern the investigation into Aidan Pitt's murder. It was more to do with the Frankie Ingram investigation.

If it was right, it wouldn't reveal the person responsible but Nathan had a feeling that it *would* reveal a significant piece of the puzzle which had, so far, eluded them.

Might as well solve part of someone else's mystery while we're waiting to get a result on the Pitt murder, thought Nathan as he drove out of the police car park. *At least it'll put a smile on Toby Carter's face.*

ooooooo

"Be quiet, Beau."

Penny Baker's Labrador, Beau, announced Nathan's arrival before sloping off in search of a cool place to flop down.

"Oh, hello. I spoke to your sidekick in London just a while ago." Penny stood to one side to let Nathan pass. "Is this quick? It's just that I'm getting ready for the memorial and I've got a lot to do."

"It's okay, I don't need to come in. I just want to ask you a question."

"Oh, right. Regarding Aidan's death?

"More to do with Frankie's, actually," said Nathan. "I'm just following up on a hunch."

"Hmmm, interesting. Okay, what is it?"

"Your house in London. Who has keys?"

"Owen and I both have a set. And we have a spare set that we lend to anyone who wants to go and stay there. Why?"

Nathan ignored the question. "And where do you keep the keys?"

"Owen keeps his on his keyring, and mine and the spare set are on a hook behind the front door with everyone else's house keys. Why?"

"What do you mean 'everyone else's house keys'? Who's everyone else?"

"Our next door neighbour, the woman over the road who looks after the dogs while we're away, Amy, Eddie, Ruby."

"You've got keys to their houses?"

"Yes, and they've all got a key to this house. Why are you asking anyway?"

"Can't tell you anything, I'm afraid, but thanks for the info—you've been *very* helpful!"

ooooooo

Ingram's Ink was in a side street in a quiet neighbourhood on the edge of town.

Strange place for a tattoo shop. Wouldn't have thought they'd get much business here, thought Nathan. As he pushed open the door, a buzzer announced his arrival but a young man with a heavily tattooed face didn't look up from the forearm he was working on.

"Be with you in a sec. Sit down in the den if you want, take the weight off. Our portfolio's on the table if you need some design ideas." He looked up. "It's just over there and— oh, I guess you're not interested in looking through our design portfolio?"

Nathan grinned. "Is it that obvious? No, I'm not here to get inked. I'd just like to have a word with someone who can answer a couple of questions. I'm DCI Costello from the St. Eves station."

"'kay. If you don't mind waiting, Josie will be back soon. She's only gone out to get some sandwiches—she won't be long. This guy's in his lunch break, see, so I've got to finish up so he can get back to work."

"That's okay, I'll wait."

Nathan sat down on a bean bag in the den. The walls were full of photographs of Frankie, and Nathan guessed that since his death, the shop had most likely become a less vibrant, quieter place without its namesake.

A pile of magazines and newspapers offered an eclectic selection of reading matter. As he flicked idly through it, it occurred to him that, apart from the tattoo design magazines, the alternative reading material was rarely, if ever, updated.

Hamburgers, Homicide and a Honeymoon

Good grief, some of this stuff's older than me. A special edition of *Hey You!* magazine covering the wedding of Prince William to Catherine Middleton looked to be the most current in the pile.

Hmm, this could be interesting. He pulled a copy of *Tats Monthly*, a magazine devoted to tattoo news, which was only a little over a year old, from the middle of the pile. The magazine's cover promised an interview with tattoo artist, Frankie Ingram, following his fourth nomination for an accolade at the International Tattoo of the Year Awards.

Nathan thumbed through the magazine until he reached the feature, the first picture of which was a full-page, colour photograph of Frankie, leaning casually against the front window of the shop, grinning widely and surrounded by all his employees, each wearing a t-shirt emblazoned with the logo *St. Eves Believes in Frankie!*

The buzzer announced the return of Josie with the sandwiches and he accosted her immediately. "Good afternoon, I'm DCI Costello." He showed her his warrant card. "Sorry, I know you're on a lunch break but this won't take long. I need to ask you a couple of questions."

"Oh, alright. Is it to do with the shop? We're all still waiting to find out what's going to happen, see. Since Frankie died, we don't know if we're going to stay open or what. I'm a key holder so I can still open up but we're still waiting to hear from his brother. He put half the money in, but he's a sleeping partner. Anyway, there's usually seven of us but since it happened, Amy and Casper have been too upset to come in to work. Not that the rest of us haven't been upset, but if we all stayed at home, who'd keep the place running? Some of us have to—"

"Look, sorry to interrupt," said Nathan. "No, it's not about the shop. It's about rotas. I assume you had rotas to let everyone when they were working, to record holidays, that sort of thing?"

Josie shook her head. "No, Frankie didn't use rotas. We just used the diary."

"Perfect. Can you tell me who was working on Friday the 17th and Saturday the 18th of March, please?"

Josie flicked back through the pages. "Okay, here we are...oh yeah, I remember now. That was the weekend Amy was away so we were short-staffed. It was a flippin' nightmare.

"Right, let's see...so Frankie was working on the Friday with me, Casper, and Giles, and on Saturday, I worked with Trinny, Casper, and Giles, and Bethany came in to do eleven till seven."

Nathan's heart sank. If Frankie had been working on the Friday, his hunch had been wrong. There was no way he could have been in London at six-thirty if he'd been working at the shop, 300 miles away.

He'd had a theory that it was Frankie the neighbour saw at the house in March. When Penny had told him that Frankie had a key to her place, Nathan wondered if he'd let himself in while Penny and Owen had been away, and helped himself to the London house key for a quick visit with a girlfriend?

Nathan didn't for a minute think that Frankie had been responsible for meddling with the hot tub—after all, why would he have jumped in first if he'd been the person responsible for causing the damage?—but he *had* hoped that his hunch would, at least, solve the mystery of who the neighbour had seen visiting the house.

It seemed, though, that his hunch was wrong. Frankie had been working on the day in question, so it can't have been him.

"So you're absolutely sure that Frankie was here on Friday the 17th?" he asked, one more time.

The phone rang and Josie excused herself as she answered it. "Afternoon, Ingram's Ink. Josie speaking."

As Nathan waited for her to finish, he flicked over the page of the magazine and his eyes fixed on the next picture of Frankie's feature. He froze as he began to process what it told him.

"Sorry about that." Josie gave him a wide smile. "So anyway, yes, Frankie was working on Friday 17th. But only until twelve-thirty."

"I'm sorry, what?"

"He was only working until twelve-thirty," said Josie. "He had the rest of the day off, see, and the Saturday, too. I remember now, thinking back, it was chaos trying to share all his appointments out between us. D'you remember, Giles? He only decided to take the time off a couple of days before, so we didn't have a lot of time to rearrange the diary."

Still clutching the magazine, Nathan was already halfway out of the front door. "Thank you, you've been very helpful. Oh, and I'm borrowing this." He held up the magazine and to his car.

He almost didn't dare to think that, at last, everything was starting to fall into place. He glanced at the headline, *Tattoo Artist Spotted with Mystery Woman in Swanky City Hotel.*

Underneath it was a picture of Frankie and a woman being besieged by a swarm of photographers, doing their best to escape from the unwanted attention in a lift. He had a protective arm around her and his other arm outstretched, fingers splayed in front of a camera lens, and she had her head down and her arms up across her face. Before the lift doors closed, the photographer had not only captured them head on, but also their reflections in the smoked glass mirrors on the walls behind them.

The tattoo on the back of Frankie's head was clearly visible.

So were the blonde tresses of hair peeking out from between the woman's black hat and the collar of her black coat.

And the large tattoo of the bunch of purple orchids on her calf.

CHAPTER 12

"To Frankie." Penny raised her glass and everyone joined her in a toast. "May he be covering the cherubs in heaven with his beautiful art. Thank you all so much for coming. I know that Frankie would be over the moon that so many of you turned out to celebrate his life—it's been a wonderful afternoon."

At the end of Frankie Ingram's memorial service at Penny and Owen's house, Charlotte was playing taxi driver.

"Thanks so much for a lovely time, Penny. Even though I didn't know Frankie very well, you made him sound so familiar, I felt like I did…we both did, didn't we?"

Jess nodded. "And it was so nice of you to invite me, even though I didn't know him at all."

"Oh, you're welcome," said Penny. "Amy and I are so glad you could come. We just wanted to fill the place with people we knew Frankie loved, and would have loved, and we're sure he would have loved both of you. You've been so kind to us.

"Well, I'm glad to see that Ruby looks so much better than I expected her to," said Charlotte. "When I saw Amy the other day she said she'd been in a terrible state."

Penny nodded. "She was, but was so determined to come to the memorial, she's been trying to manage without the pills. The doctor told her to only take one if she really needs it to help her sleep. And she's eaten quite a bit this afternoon, which is more than she's done for days, so that'll help."

"Well, if she does suddenly get tired, at least she only has to go up the stairs to bed," said Charlotte.

"Oh no," said Penny. "Ruby's not staying here now—she's been at Amy's since yesterday." She looked embarrassed. "To tell you the truth, I'm relieved. I don't want any negative vibes around Zac and it was all getting pretty intense with her staying here. I mean, I love her to death, but I mentioned it to Amy and she offered Ruby a place at her apartment. She's done us all a favour by letting her stay there—it's like an oasis of calm, which is just what Ruby needs to get herself together.

"We've got a toddler and dogs, so the antithesis of quiet!" She looked at her watch. "Anyway, if you'll excuse me, I must get off and give Zac his bath. Thanks again for coming, Amy! Charlotte and Jess are leaving now if you want to say goodbye."

A red-nosed Amy approached. "Thanks for coming, both of you. Frankie would have been so chuffed that so many people turned up. It's just such a shame that Eddie couldn't be here 'cos he loved Frankie to bits but something came up and he had to go and visit his mum."

Charlotte nodded. "Well, I'm sure he was thinking about him." She knew that, after Eddie's confession to Nathan about the fake blackmail attempt, and his mother's confession to the police about David Travis' murder, he'd gone to stay at her place until she found out what her fate would be for withholding evidence in a murder investigation, and it was still being debated whether he, himself, would face any charges. She wondered how much he'd told Amy.

Amy wiped her eyes and blew her nose. "We're going back to my place now—I think Ruby needs to get to bed. She's a lot better than she was but she's ever so tired…hang on, I'll call her over. Ruby! *Rubes!* Come and say goodbye while I go and get our coats."

"Thanks for coming to say goodbye to Frankie," said Ruby, hugging Charlotte and Jess. "He loved life, he really did. He loved life, and I loved him… I mean, we *all* did. It wasn't right that he died. It wasn't his time. But I know his death will be avenged." She smiled and shrugged her shoulders. "Who knows, maybe even tonight."

"Right." Amy reappeared with the coats. "Come on, Rubes. It's time we went home, I think. Thanks again for making time for Frankie," she said to Charlotte and Jess. "It means so much to all of us. I hope we'll see you again soon." She linked her arm in Ruby's and they disappeared through the dispersing crowd.

"She knows his death will be avenged?" said Jess. "What the hell's she talking about?"

"I think that might have been the medication talking," said Charlotte. "She must still have some of it in her system, even if she hasn't taken any today. Poor thing, I feel sorry for her."

On the way out to the car, a tattooed DJ who'd played Frankie's favourite music throughout the afternoon was talking loudly on his phone.

"Oh, you're kidding! I've got a gig to get to at *The Bottle of Beer* on the marina. How the hell am I going to get there? Why didn't you call me earlier?"

"Wonder what that's all about?" said Jess.

"Don't know, but I'm about to find out." Charlotte tapped the man on the shoulder.

"'Scuse me, I wasn't earwigging, but I just overheard your phone call. We're on our way back to St. Eves town centre. Has something happened?"

"There's been an accident on the main road into town," said the DJ. "That was my wife—she's been stuck in traffic for over an hour."

"Oh, I hope it's not serious—has anyone been hurt?"

"Don't think so. A lorry jack-knifed and it's blocked both lanes of the dual carriageway. No injuries, according to the reports, just a lot of very irritable drivers. Anyway, the traffic's nose to tail all the way into and out of town, so if you're going that way be prepared for a very long delay." The DJ walked off, his phone to his ear.

"Well, I don't know about you," said Charlotte, "but I don't fancy sitting in that for hours. What about you?"

"Not really. How about we have a drink somewhere?" said Jess. "Hopefully, the traffic will clear soon."

They walked down the main street, past pubs, coffee shops and wine bars until a small bistro caught their eye. It was strung with lights, and candles on the tables inside gave it a cosy glow.

"How about here?" said Charlotte.

Jess nodded. "Looks perfect."

They'd barely sat down at a table when a voice called out, "Charlotte! Tess! Is that you? It's us! Over here!"

Cindy Powell, Brenda Tatum, and four other women were sitting at a table on the other side of the bistro, sharing two large pepperoni pizzas.

"Oh no! If I have to look at one more photograph of Aidan Pitt…" Charlotte whispered out of the corner of her mouth.

"I swear, if she calls me Tess one more time…" Jess whispered back.

"Hello, we thought it was you," said Cindy, taking a large bite out of a slice of pizza.

"Fancy seeing you here," said Jess.

"We've just held a vigil near Aidan's house. Just a few members this time because it's the weekend and people have other things to do. And then we found out there's been an accident on the road back into town so we're sitting here killing time. Care to join us?"

For the next half hour, Cindy, Brenda, and the rest of *The Pittettes* exhibited their impressive recollection of virtually every move Aidan Pitt had made over the past years.

While their stories kept each other entertained, Charlotte and Jess were bored stiff.

"My cheeks are killing me," whispered Jess. "Forcing yourself to smile for thirty minutes isn't easy, you know."

"I'm going to try Nathan again. Tell him I'll be late back." Charlotte dialled the number but got a message that there was no signal. She tried three more times with the same result. "Can't get him. I'll try again in a bit. I bet he's—" She stopped talking, suddenly aware of the conversation that was going on across the table.

"Anyway, I much prefer her hair when it's blonde. Although it's a beautiful colour, the brown is much too dark for her skin tone; it makes her look washed out. I hate to speak ill of Aidan, but it was very unfair of him to ask her to do it, I think."

"Who are we talking about now?" asked Jess, trying to involve herself in the conversation.

"Ruby Pitt," said Cindy. "I was just saying how I prefer her original hair colour, but Aidan asked her to change it because he thought she was getting too much attention as a blonde. So she coloured it dark brown, which is gorgeous, but not on her."

"The thing is," said Brenda, "she likes it blonde so, every now and then, she changes it back. It used to be a constant battle between the two of them."

"All the colour changes have been terribly bad for her hair, though," said Cindy, chewing on her pizza. "All that colouring and bleaching and colouring and bleaching has left it so thin. She goes to see a top trichologist in London about it, apparently."

"Yes, that's why she wears a hat so often," said Cindy.

Charlotte felt like she'd been smacked in the face as everything started to clear in her mind.

Events that had been foggy and jumbled became vivid as she gained clarity of thought. She closed her eyes and as she recalled the events on the day of Frankie's death, Big Al's words suddenly came into her head: "Sometimes you just gotta look at the bigger picture to see what's going on right under your nose."

She gasped as she remembered the most vital clue; the one she'd unwittingly been keeping to herself for so long, which had been coaxed out by Cindy's recent revelation.

Hamburgers, Homicide and a Honeymoon

As she thought back to Penny and Owen's barbecue that afternoon in London, everything became un-muddled.

She'd been swinging back and forth on the bench seat with Ruby, and everyone had been chatting and laughing at Amy and Frankie's dash to the hot tub, Amy trying her best to overtake and get in first.

After that, everything had happened so quickly and so close together that Charlotte hadn't been able to separate events in her muddled mind but now, they were crystal clear.

The swing had abruptly stopped, and she'd heard a single, strangled scream—muted amongst the laughter—immediately followed by a splash as Frankie had jumped into the tub. After that, *everyone* had begun to scream as the afternoon descended into chaos.

But the first scream had come *before* Frankie jumped.

It had come from Ruby.

She'd stopped the swing and let out that repressed scream when she realised Frankie was about to jump to his death.

She'd screamed because she'd known the hot tub was dangerous. And the only reason she'd known the hot tub was dangerous must have been because she was the person who'd made it that way.

Charlotte's mind raced as she slotted all the pieces together. She was almost sure she had an explanation for why the screwdriver that had been used to damage the hot tub had been put back in its box.

It was because of Ruby's OCD, she was sure of it.

She recalled the proverb Ruby had said her father used to drum into her and her siblings when they were young: 'A place for everything and everything in its place.'

Ruby had to put the screwdriver back in its box, along with all the rest of them, because her OCD wouldn't allow her not to, but she obviously never thought it would link her to Frankie's murder.

Of course, she hadn't intended to kill Frankie... because she loved him.

Charlotte thought back to what Ruby had told her just an hour ago. *'He loved life, and I loved him.'*

She'd been in love with Frankie. That's why she was taking his death so hard.

Charlotte was convinced that Ruby and Frankie were the couple the neighbour had seen during that weekend in March—when Ruby's hair was blonde.

It all made sense.

But Ruby had obviously planned to kill someone. If not Frankie, then who?

A shiver ran right through her when the answer came to her. When she remembered Penny telling her at the party that Amy 'always has to be the first one in the tub'.

"Oh my goodness!" She bolted up from her chair, spilling her tea all over the tablecloth.

"What is it? You haven't got wind again, have you?" said Jess, jumping up with her.

"No, no. What was it that Ruby said again? About being avenged?"

"Erm, something about knowing that Frankie's death will be avenged. Maybe tonight," said Jess. "Why? What's going on?"

"Look, we have to get hold of Nathan. Or Ben or Fiona, or someone at the station. They have to get to Amy's apartment. I'll call Penny, you try Nathan."

"Well, I've got Ben here. What do you want me to tell him?"

"Tell him to get hold of Nathan and get to Amy Baker's ASAP or they'll have another body on their hands!"

ooooooo

"Oh dear! Just when I thought I was all cried out." Amy wiped her face on her sleeve. "Have you got any more tissues?"

Ruby opened her handbag. "Here, take the pack."

"Thanks." Amy blew her nose and recoiled at her reflection in the mirror on her lipstick case. "Oh, gross." She leaned against the window of the taxi and wrote 'Frankie' in the condensation left by her breath. As she watched it disappear in the light cast by the streetlamps, she began to cry again. "Oh, Rubes, I need a hug."

Ruby held out her arm and Amy snuggled down next to her. "That's better," she said, and closed her eyes.

In the darkness of the taxi, Ruby's lips curled in a humourless, malevolent smile as she stroked Amy's hair.

"There, there, Amy, love. I've got you now, I've got you…"

ooooooo

"Rubes, you left your wedding and engagement rings in the bathroom." Amy called out through the bedroom door. "I'll leave them on the kitchen table, okay?" She ran downstairs, feeling a little better for having had a shower.

Page 193

She heard Ruby's footsteps on the stairs. "I'm making a cup of tea—you want one? *Ruby!* Do you want a cup—" She turned to see her friend standing in the kitchen doorway. "Oh, you're here. Do you want a cup of tea?"

Ruby said nothing.

"Look, I've been going on all day about how upset I am," said Amy, "but I can't *imagine* how upset you must be. You've lost a friend *and* your husband, haven't you? Listen, why don't you come and sit down and let me get you a proper drink? What would you like? Wine, gin and tonic…oh no, better not with the meds. Tell you what, we'll stick with tea, shall we? Come on, sit down and I'll keep you company. I'll get a box of tissues and we can sit and talk about Frankie and Aidan. It might make us feel bett— er, what's that in your hand?"

Ruby had changed into a bathrobe, the object she held at her side hidden in its folds.

"What's up, Ruby? You look a little strange, like—"

"Shut up, Amy! And sit down… NOW!"

Amy dropped into a chair immediately. "Ruby! You're scaring me. What's wrong?"

"D'you know what?" Ruby sat opposite her. "I am so *sick* of hearing your voice, endlessly whingeing on and on about how *you* feel because Frankie died. About how *your* life will never be the same. About how close *you* were to Frankie. You're a selfish, spoilt brat. All you ever think about is yourself. As long as you're okay, you couldn't care less about anyone else, could you?"

"Ruby, I'm s-sorry," stuttered Amy. "I had no idea you felt that way. Please, I didn't mean to be selfish. I

Hamburgers, Homicide and a Honeymoon

should have been more sympathetic. I know how upset you've been about Aidan, and I haven't been very supportive, have I?"

Ruby laughed. "Upset about *Aidan*? Why on earth would I be upset about Aidan? I killed him!" She raised the object in her hand above her head and brought it down on the table in front of her with a crash.

Amy gasped when she saw the bronze statuette from Aidan's office, bearing the plaque, 'Triathlon Champion 2012', the plinth on which it stood splattered with dried blood. Her hands flew to her mouth. "No! No, Ruby. You didn't?"

Ruby laughed. "Yep, I did. It was little old me."

"But how could it have been?" said Amy. "You said you left home *before* Aidan was killed."

"Yeah, I did. But then I went back again," said Ruby, running her fingers over the statue. "I left early, hung around outside for a while and then sneaked back inside. When I heard Aidan go upstairs, I crept into his study and took the trophy from his desk. Poor love, he didn't know what hit him. Literally!" She laughed again but Amy saw that her eyes were dull.

"Oh dear, poor Amy. You have no idea what all this is about, do you? You really have no idea. Think about it—think back to London. Who's *normally* the first one in the hot tub? You. Every bloody year, it's you. Why couldn't it have been you *this* year? It wasn't *supposed* to be Frankie! Damn it, Amy—why'd you have to go and ruin everything?"

Amy's mouth fell open, and she shrank back in her chair as realised the significance of Ruby's words. "It

Page 195

was *you* who tampered with the hot tub? *You* disabled the safety mechanisms to kill *me*?"

"Yes, Amy. It was me. I did it when you went to France with Penny, and the guys went off on their weekend jolly. I let myself into your sister's house and borrowed the keys for London. I went with Frankie for the weekend."

"Frankie was in on it?" whimpered Amy.

Ruby rolled her eyes. "Don't be ridiculous, he had no idea. And he'd hardly have jumped in if he'd known what was going to happen, would he? No, Frankie was sleeping when I rigged the tub. And you shouldn't sound so surprised. When you know what you're looking for, you can find information about anything you like on the internet. It's easy—especially for a researcher, like me."

"So *you* were the blonde woman and Frankie was the man?" said Amy. "Oh, my God, we thought Elsie was imagining things. Even with you changing your hair colour every five minutes, we never for one minute thought it could be you." She blinked rapidly. "But why would you want to kill *me*?"

"Oh, come on, Amy. Why do you think? I'm sure you won't have to think too hard."

The heat rose in Amy's cheeks. "Because of me and Aidan?"

Ruby gave her a slow handclap. "Oh, bravo. Ten out of ten. What, you think I didn't know? Don't flatter yourself, love, you weren't the only one. I knew about all his floozies. The rest didn't bother me so much, though 'cos they weren't pretending to be my friends.

"God, you make me sick—you act like butter wouldn't melt in your mouth, but you think nothing of taking my husband to bed while you're supposed to be a friend of mine. How could you do that? Did you honestly think I was going to let you carry on under my nose and do nothing?

"I've been waiting for this moment for months. I know how long you were having an affair with Aidan. How do you think I felt when I found out, Amy? How could you have done that? How many times were we in each other's company while you were having an affair with my husband? And how do you think I felt when I found out he'd bought you this apartment with *our* money?" A solitary tear forced its way out of the corner of her eye.

"I've hated you for so long. But do you know what made me hate you most of all? I hated you for being able to grieve for Frankie when I couldn't. Don't you think Aidan would have found it strange if I'd been too upset? I had to keep my emotions bottled up. You think these tears I've been crying since Aidan's death are for him? They're not. They're for Frankie. Because I loved *him*. We were supposed to be together. This wasn't supposed to happen. I couldn't even spend what turned out to be his last days with him, because Aidan insisted on coming to London at the last minute and ruined it all."

Amy frowned. "You and *Frankie*? You mean you and Frankie went to the house that weekend as... as more than friends?"

"Oh, please, don't be so naïve," said Ruby. "Of course we were more than friends. We were lovers."

"I can't believe it," said Amy. "He and I were so close but he never told me. He never said a word. I mean, I knew you were really good friends, but—" Her gaze dropped to Ruby's hand and she stared. She stared at Ruby's wedding ring finger without its wedding and engagement rings.

It bore a tattoo that said, 'We Are One.'

"It was you!" Amy gasped. "You were the other half to Frankie's tattoo! 'Together…We Are One.' Oh, Ruby, I had no idea. He wouldn't tell me who it was. Why didn't you tell me?"

Ruby's eyebrows shot up. "Why didn't I tell *you*? Why do you think, Amy? Because Aidan was so addicted to you by the time I fell in love with Frankie, it was as though I didn't exist. Of all people, do you really think I would have come to *you*?" she said, incredulously. "Oh, believe me, I wanted to tell someone—I wanted to shout it from the rooftops but I had to keep it to myself. I tried to resist Frankie for so long, I really did, but in the end, when I couldn't make Aidan love me, no matter what I did, I just couldn't help myself."

A knock at the door startled them.

"Amy. It's DCI Costello. Can you open the door, please?"

"What's he doing here?" Ruby hissed. "Did you call him?"

"How am I supposed to have called him, for God's sake? I've been sitting here with you."

The door opened slowly. "Ruby, it's Penny. I'm not going to come in, I'm just telling you it's me, okay? Is Amy okay?"

"Yes, I'm okay, Pen! Please get me out of here." Amy shrieked as Ruby raised the trophy above her head.

"*Ruby!* Put it down," said Nathan, standing in the doorway. "Put the trophy down."

"Why are you blaming me?" said Ruby. "Blame her. If Amy hadn't let Frankie get in the hot tub before her, he'd still be alive."

"Yes, but she'd be dead, wouldn't she?" Nathan took a step forward. "Just like you'd planned. Now give me the trophy, Ruby."

For a moment, it seemed as though she was going to relent but then she ran at Amy with a cry, the bloodied plinth of the statuette swinging wildly as Amy dodged left and right to avoid it. As Ruby backed her into a corner and raised the statuette one last time, Nathan launched himself at her from halfway across the room and knocked her off-balance.

She was so wild, it took both Nathan and Fiona to restrain and cuff her. With her eyes wild and her breathing heavy, she spat and swore at Amy. "You'd better get used to looking over your shoulder, because I promise you, I'm going to be back to finish you off when you least expect it."

As Fiona prised the statuette from Ruby's fingers, she said, "And I promise *you*, you won't be back to finish anything off. Not where you're going."

Nathan picked up the statuette and dropped it into an evidence bag.

He had the result he'd been waiting for.
He had Aidan's killer.
He had Frankie's killer.
It was over.

Epilogue

"So, Ruby Pitt killed the tattoo artist accidentally, but her husband intentionally? And she was in love with the tattoo artist? And her husband was in love with one of her best friends? And that friend was the intended victim in the hot tub accident that killed the tattoo artist? And the assistant who'd worked for Aidan Pitt for years was the son he never knew existed?"

Garrett shook his head. "Good grief, I'm glad I'm a fisherman, Nathan—it's a lot less complicated! Talk about enough material for an entire soap opera season. And this one here figured it all out?"

Garrett Walton hugged his goddaughter, taking care not to squeeze too tightly.

"I keep telling her, she's a natural," said Nathan, with a grin. "I could put her on a case right now and I bet she'd have the bad guys in handcuffs before some of the other officers had finished scratching their heads."

"And I keep telling *you*, stop putting all these crazy ideas into her head!" said Laura, wagging her finger at Nathan. "I prefer knowing that my goddaughter's safe and sound, indoors and surrounded by people who love her. Not out pounding the pavements, having to deal with goodness knows what."

"Laura, I don't think I'll be squeezing myself into a WPC uniform any time soon, so you can stop worrying." Charlotte gave her baby bump a loving pat. "And, even if I did want to join the force, which I don't, I doubt I'd have the time for the next, oh, eighteen years or so!"

"Well, that's a relief, love," said Laura. "I can't help but worry sometimes that one day, we'll take a walk down to the marina, find a 'For Sale' sign on the door of *Charlotte's Plaice*, and you patrolling the neighbourhood on a police issue bicycle, in a pair of ugly police issue shoes, with a truncheon and a pair of handcuffs your only concessions to fashion accessories."

Charlotte giggled. "Oh don't be daft! If I was going to sell up, you'd be one of the first to know!"

"Well, I certainly hope you won't sell up," said Leo, whose lap was playing host to a very relaxed Pippin. "Harry and I would starve."

"Hear, hear! I'll second that!" Harry touched his pint of beer to Leo's.

On a sunny Saturday afternoon in July, Charlotte had opened the café for a private party. Garrett and Laura, Jess and Ben, Harriett and Leo, Ava, Betty, Harry and Lola had all been invited for a long, lazy lunch.

She'd been struggling with being on her feet all day at the café, so the following Friday would be her last full day at work until well after the baby was born and, until she gave up for good, she'd be sharing the shifts with Laura—fifty-fifty.

Before then, though, she wanted to make the effort to cook a delicious lunch for her friends and family, and today was the only day that everyone could get together at the same time.

"Hi, sorry we're late!" Jess and Ben arrived with flowers, Champagne and sparkling apple juice for Charlotte. "I bought sparkling for a change so you don't feel left out when we open the bubbly," said Jess as she threw her arms around her friend's shoulders.

"Lovely, thank you! Ooh, and it's chilled, too. Anyone fancy a glass of Champagne now? Yes? Right, can you do the honours, please Nathan. You know how useless I am at opening those bottles."

The corks popped and the friends relaxed in each other's company—warmed by the sun in the turquoise sky, and cooled by the breeze that caused the wind chimes that hung from the masts to tinkle and clatter. *Better than any music*, thought Charlotte, happily.

"These burger appetisers are delicious, Charlotte," said Betty. "Where did you find such small buns?"

"I made them. I don't normally make my own burger buns but I couldn't find any that small and I just wanted the burgers to be bite-sized, so I made them."

"They've got a wonderful flavour," said Harriett. "Not like anything I've ever tasted before. Very interesting."

"Good, I'm glad you like them. Right, I'll just go and check on lunch. I won't be a sec."

"Do you need a hand, dear?" asked Ava

"No, I'm okay, thanks. You just relax and enjoy yourself."

"Well, if there's anything I can do, just give me a shout. I'm very versatile, you know. I can turn my hand to most things."

"Okay, will do, but I'm sure I'll manage." Charlotte smiled and took her glass of non-alcoholic fizz into the kitchen.

"Right." She spoke to herself as she crossed off things from the to-do list on the counter. "Now let me see...starters are all ready, desserts are done. I just need to check on the turbot."

She rubbed her back. The twinges she'd experienced in the past had been bothering her again over the last few days but, although the pain was quite intense, it didn't last long as the twinges came and went. In any case, at her check-up four days before, the midwife had told her that everything was fine so she wasn't in the slightest bit worried about them.

But as she bent to open the oven door, she was overcome by the most intense pain she'd ever felt. She almost passed out it was so strong. She tried to straighten up but couldn't. Her instincts told her this was no false alarm. This wasn't wind or constipation. Doubled up and unable to move, she found her voice and shouted for help.

"Nathan! NATHAN! Help! Someone, heeeelp! I think the baby's coming!"

ooooooo

"Where *is* that bloody ambulance?" Nathan held Charlotte's hand and dabbed her forehead with a cold towel. He felt sick with worry but was keeping calm for Charlotte's sake.

Her contractions were closer together now but, as relaxed as she was trying to stay, concern was etched all over her face. "Nathan, if it doesn't get here soon, I'm going to have this baby on the kitchen floor."

"I thought first babies took hours to be born?" said Betty.

"I think that's more usual but they can come very quickly, too," said Lola. "Looks like Charlotte's going to fall into the latter category."

"It's early—it's not due until the 11th of August," said Nathan, rubbing the small of Charlotte's back as she tried to find a comfortable position. "Is that okay?"

"Well, it's not hugely early," said Lola. "I know people who have had babies far earlier and they've been perfectly okay with the right care. The hospital will look after Charlotte and the baby, so try not to worry too much."

"Do you think Garrett, Ben, Harry and I have got time to take Pippin for a walk?" Leo called, from the bar. "I think he needs to pee."

Harriett stuck her head through the serving hatch in the wall to speak to him. "What do you mean? Have you got time?"

"Well, we don't want to miss anything," said Leo. "We want to be here when the paramedics arrive so we can cheer Charlotte on."

"'Cheer her on?'" Harriett clicked her tongue. "She's having a baby, Leo, not racing a horse. Yes, go on, but don't go too far and *don't* be too long."

As Laura held onto one of Charlotte's hands and Lola held the other, Ava was busy boiling kettles and pans for hot water.

"What are you doing?" asked Jess.

"Getting ready to deliver this baby, that's what I'm doing," said Ava. "Hopefully, we won't have to but it pays to be prepared." Amidst the chaos, she was so calm it was as if delivering babies was something she did every day. "There are enough of us here who've had one, for goodness' sake, I'm sure we can manage between us if necessary. Now, where are the clean tea towels, dear?"

"Oh, now wait a minute. I'm not sure about that, Ava," said Nathan. "I know you mean well but I'd really rather wait for the ambulance. No disrespect, but the paramedics are qualified at this." He looked at his watch.

"Where *are* they? It's been almost ten minutes since we called."

Ava tapped a foot, one hand planted on a hip. "Nathan, I've no doubt that *you'd* like to wait for the ambulance but perhaps you should consider what *Charlotte* wants to do? I'm not one for interfering, as you well know, but don't you think this should be her decision?"

She crouched down and stroked Charlotte's sweat-drenched cheek. "What do you say, my dear? Would you like us to give it a go if you need us to?"

Charlotte looked at the faces around her—Jess, Laura, Ava, Harriett, Betty, Aunt Lola and Nathan. Almost all the people she loved most in the world. She wanted the paramedics to look after her but if they couldn't get to her in time, she knew she couldn't wish for anyone better to try to help her.

She nodded. "Okay, if needs be."

Ava squeezed her hand. "Good girl. Right, let's get organised."

ooooooo

"Nathan Costello, I swear, you are never coming near me again!" Charlotte dug her nails into his hand and she panted through a contraction.

"Ow, your nails are sharp!"

"Oh. *Are* they indeed? I'm so awfully sorry." Charlotte glared up at him, unable to keep the sarcasm from her voice. "Did I *hurt* you? Are you in *pain*?" She looked around at her friends. "Can someone throttle Nathan, please?"

Jess grinned at Laura. "He'll be saying he needs a cup of tea and a lie down, next."

"Oh, good Lord!" Ava exclaimed.

"What is it?" said Nathan. "*Ava!*"

"This is all happening so quickly, she said. "Right, Harriett, pass me some more towels please, and that pan of hot water. Charlotte, the baby's head's almost here so I need you to stop pushing and pant. It won't be easy, I know, but try hard. I'll tell you when to push again, alright?"

Charlotte nodded. "Ava, I'm scared."

"I know you are, dear, but just focus on me and you'll be fine. Let's see if we can make this the most wonderful experience of your life, shall we?"

"We're back!" Leo called out. "Did we miss anything?"

"No, looks like you got back just in time," said Harriett.

"Any sign of that ambulance out there?" said Nathan. "I just called them again and they said they're two minutes away."

"No, didn't see it but you know what the traffic's like on a Saturday—oh, hang on, this must be it."

The sound of a siren got louder and louder, then stopped.

"Oh, thank God," said Nathan. "Charlotte, it's here."

"We can't wait for them, I'm afraid, this baby's about to be born." Ava, who rarely showed emotion, blinked away the tears. "Right, Charlotte, focus on me and give me one more big push, alright? Come on, dear, you can do it."

Accompanied by rousing cheers from Garrett, Leo, Harry and Ben, Charlotte and Nathan's baby was born. As everyone else burst into tears, the paramedics arrived.

"Someone called for an ambulance?"

"They're in there, mate," said Garrett, as a feeble wail, growing in volume with every second, heralded the arrival of the newest addition to the Costello family. "But it sounds like you missed all the action."

"Blimey, you've had an audience, haven't you love?" The paramedics took over as Nathan lifted Ava off her feet and hugged her. "Ava, if I live to be a hundred, I will never be able to thank you enough."

"Oh, get away with you," said Ava, wiping her eyes. "Go and enjoy your new baby."

As the medics tended to Charlotte and the baby, she heard her aunt whisper to Laura. "Oh, how I wish Scott and Molly were here. They'd be the proudest grandparents."

Charlotte bit her lip. Her parents had been with her all through this—they were always with her, she knew that—but if she'd ever wanted a hug from them, it was now.

As the paramedic handed the baby back to her, she held it close and let all the emotions out.

ooooooo

"Well, I don't think I've ever seen a mother or baby in better shape, all things considered!" The midwife at the hospital peered into the baby blanket cocoon that Charlotte was holding. "Congratulations to both of you, and I'll drop by and see you and baby tomorrow."

"I suppose we'd better get home, then," said Nathan. "There'll be a lot of people who want to come and visit but I think we should put them off for a while, don't you? So we can have some time together, just the three of us."

"Yes, I think that's a good idea," said Charlotte. "But could you collect Pippin from Leo's? I'd like to introduce him to the baby as soon as possible."

"Okay, I'll drop you home and then I'll call round and pick him up. Come on, let's go."

After twenty minutes of struggling to put the baby seat in the back of the car, they set off on the short drive home.

"What do you think about the names we talked about?" said Charlotte. "Do you think the one we chose fits?

Nathan nodded. "I think it's perfect."

She smiled. "That's good. I do, too."

"Right, I'll come in and get you settled and then I'll go and get Pippin." Nathan pulled up at the cottage and helped Charlotte inside before hugging her and kissing the baby. "Won't be long."

It was quiet and still. As she lifted the sleeping baby from the seat and held it close to her, Charlotte knew this was probably the last time the cottage would be that way.

She sat down on the large bay window seat in the living room—with its view of the sea, it was the place in the cottage she loved most.

"So, it's just you and me for a little while," she said, kissing the top of her baby's head and inhaling its newborn scent. "Daddy and Pippin will be home soon and, in a day or two, you'll meet all our friends and family. You'll have to wait a little while longer to meet Grandpa George, Grandma Hattie and Aunty Barbara, though. Mind you, I expect they'll be straight on a plane when they hear about you." She smiled.

"But, before you meet anyone else, there are two people I want to introduce you to first. I'll tell you all about them when you're older. I'll tell you that even though you can't see them, they'll always be with you…always be beside you."

"They won't ever be here to hold your hand, or pick you up when you fall, or tell you they love you, so *I'm* telling you—if they were here, they would love you more than anything in the world."

She looked out at the sea, and the sand on which she and her parents had enjoyed so many good times when she'd been young. She couldn't think of a better place to bring up her child.

She opened up the blanket and lifted the sleeping baby onto the crook of her arm.

"Mum, Dad. I'd like you to meet Molly Costello."

The End

Thanks for reading. I hope you enjoyed this book. If you'd like to receive notifications of my new releases, please join my Readers' Group at https://sherribryan.com

Details of my other books are on page 227 but, as a preview of what's to come, the start of the next book in the series is on the next page.

Crab Cakes, Killers and a Kaftan – Book 6

Prologue

Malcolm, the Siamese cat, watched from his position on the windowsill as his owner, Sadie Grey, slid off her bar stool and wobbled towards the door of the pub, the back of her tie-dyed kaftan caught up in one leg of her underwear.

"And don't come back until you're ready to apologise!"

With almost forty years of experience as a publican, Keith Brady was well-accustomed to dealing with clientele who'd over-indulged on alcohol. He'd dealt with verbally abusive customers, overly-affectionate customers, customers who wanted to fight the world and customers who simply fell asleep at the bar.

Sadie Grey, however, was in a class all of her own. Not only had she insulted every one of the friends who'd gathered to celebrate the success of her latest book, but she'd hurled abuse at other customers, taken a swing at Keith, and thrown up three glasses of Champagne and the half a bottle of sherry she'd quaffed before arriving at the pub, down the front of his shirt

As she reached the door, she turned and made an offensive hand gesture before straightening her kaftan and staggering out onto the pavement.

"Do you think we should see her home?" Jane Robertson's nasally voice broke the silence.

"No, I don't!" spluttered Norman—President of the cricket club, ex-head teacher of the local secondary school, and Jane's husband. "With any luck, the streetlights will cut out and she'll fall down that bloody great hole in the road outside her house…and good riddance to her!" His shoulders visibly tensed as he crossed his arms across his chest and stared at his pint of bitter, jaw clenched.

"Norm! That's a terrible thing to say." Sadie's most devoted friend, Jane, chewed nervously on her bottom lip as she took a bottle of essential oil out of her handbag and massaged a couple of drops into her temples to keep her stress headache at bay.

She tolerated Sadie's drinking and forgave her inexcusable behaviour because she knew how traumatised Sadie had been since being discarded like an old newspaper by the only man she'd ever loved. "You know what a difficult time she's had recently."

"*Recently*?! Good grief, woman! When are you going to stop making excuses for her? It was over thirty years ago she got dumped but you *will* insist on talking about it as though it only happened last week."

"You know, I bet not a day goes by that he doesn't thank his lucky stars for escaping her clutches." Rick Kagan opened a bag of salt and vinegar crisps and dipped one into his shandy. "She really can be the most awful witch sometimes."

Keith returned, fastening the buttons of a clean shirt. "I can't help thinking that I'm partly to blame for this fiasco. I should never have given her that second glass of wine, she was so obviously three sheets to the wind already, but everything was going so well I never imagined the party would end like this."

"Keith Brady, don't you *dare* blame yourself!" His indignant wife, Beverley, called from the other side of the bar where she was deep in conversation with Rick's wife,

Cathy. "The only person to blame for Sadie's appalling behaviour is Sadie. I'm so glad I was in the ladies' room when she made a spectacle of herself—I don't think I'd have been responsible for my actions if I hadn't been.

"I mean, I can understand she's not happy that none of us are in agreement with her but, really, what on earth did she expect our reaction to be when she told us her next project is going to be a semi-autobiographical exposé that includes all of us?" She shook her head and brought her Champagne flute to her coral-pink lips.

"Exactly," agreed Cathy. "Keith, Norm, and Rick are respected members of the community now." She checked her reflection in the mirror behind the bar, admiring the effects of her latest round of Botox. "The last thing we want is a book being published that spills the beans on what we all got up to when we were young. Even if she does use pseudonyms, everyone knows we've all been friends since we were kids—they're bound to work out who the book's about. For heaven's sake, Rick's constituents would never be able to look at him in the same light again."

Local government councillor, Rick, dunked another crisp into his shandy and stared ahead, lost in his thoughts. "You know, we'd all had a little too much to drink by the time she dropped the bombshell. We all said some things we shouldn't have but it was just the alcohol talking. If we sat down with Sadie and explained our reservations, rationally, I'm sure she'd understand why we'd rather the book wasn't published."

"Or even *written*, by the sound of it." Sadie's long-suffering live-in housekeeper-cum-proof-reader, Ellie Joseph, drained the remainder of her blackcurrant and lemonade. "Right, I'm off to see if she's okay." She hooked her arms through the straps of her backpack. "Honestly, you lot are worse than a bunch of kids when you all get together." She blew out a breath that rattled her lips and, shaking her head, set off for home.

"Oh dear, I do hate all this bad feeling. You don't think we were a little harsh, do you, Norm? On Sadie, I mean?" Jane bent to stroke Malcolm as he mewled and brushed against her legs.

"No, I *do not*. Not harsh enough, if you ask me." Norman wagged a fat finger at his wife. "Listen, I didn't take early retirement to spend it worrying about my reputation being ruined by Sadie Grey. If you think I'm going to sit back and do nothing, you don't know me very well, woman." He swilled the last of his pint and wiped his hand across his mouth. "Right, who's in for another round? We need to put our heads together and figure out a game plan because if that book gets published, we're done for."

ooooooo

"Sadie, it's me. Are you okay?"

Ellie slipped her backpack off her shoulders as she called upstairs.

"Sadie! You up there?"

She tutted. It wouldn't be the first time she'd come home to find Sadie sleeping off the effects of too much alcohol. Ever since the man she loved had made his indifference to her abundantly clear, she'd lost no time in seeking solace at the bottom of a bottle and now, she couldn't get through the day without a drink. A lot of her friends had drifted away after she'd started drinking—

they couldn't deal with her moods, her temper tantrums and her wretched desire to flounder in self-pity.

Ellie didn't have to live-in. She would have much preferred to move in with her boyfriend, Bradley. He lived in St. Eves, on the other side of town, but Sadie relied on her so much, it was easier to just stay with her during the week and see Bradley at weekends.

She loved spending time at Bradley's place. They'd have breakfast in bed and read the papers from cover to cover before going off for a long walk along the coastline. Afternoons were spent browsing around antique or flea markets, followed by an early evening salsa class and a visit to a local restaurant for dinner. Ellie lived for her weekends. They were what kept her going through the rest of the week.

It wasn't that she hated living-in at Sadie's but, because she did, she'd seen every side of the temperamental author.

There was no doubt she could be charming and funny—even kind at times—but, mostly, Ellie didn't like what she saw. She'd had to bite her tongue too many times to prevent herself from flying at her employer in a rage, but she'd kept her cool, primarily, for two reasons. One, the money was good and two, she was the sole beneficiary of Sadie's considerable fortune.

She knew that Sadie couldn't do without her. She'd been so disorganised when Ellie had arrived but now, everything worked like a dream. The systems she'd put in place ensured that Sadie never forgot an appointment and always knew what she had to do, and when she had to do it by. And since Ellie had come to work for her she'd never missed a deadline, which she'd been prone to do prior to her arrival, which had improved her relationship with her editor immeasurably.

The only thing Ellie couldn't do for Sadie was stop her drinking. She'd told her more times than she cared to recall that she'd never find peace of mind at the bottom of a bottle and when she'd suggested Alcoholics Anonymous, Sadie had insisted she didn't need them because she wasn't an alcoholic.

The times she'd been on the verge of moving out of Sadie's and moving in with Bradley had been many. But every time she'd packed a bag, she'd unpacked it just as quickly. It wasn't *just* the money—she felt duty-bound to stay and see that Sadie was okay.

As she climbed the stairs, she hoped that she wouldn't find Sadie in an argumentative mood. The last thing she wanted was a row.

The bedroom door was ajar and Ellie knocked gently before pushing it open. "Sadie…it's me. Oh, for heaven's sake! What's wrong?"

Sitting on the bed with tears streaming down her cheeks, Sadie was a pitiful sight. "I don't think I can take much more. Nobody wants me. *He* didn't want me and now my friends don't want me…what am I to do?" Her shoulders heaved with silent sobs.

"Listen. Of course your friends want you, you daft thing." Ellie crouched down and mopped away the tears with the sleeve of her jumper. "They're just a bit anxious because you're threatening to write about stuff they'd prefer never saw the light of day. Surely you can understand that?"

Sadie shrugged a shoulder. "I thought they'd be pleased. It's not every day that a best-selling author offers to put you in her book, you know."

"But they don't *want* to be in it. I've no idea what you all got up to when you were young but it's pretty obvious they don't want it out there for the world and his wife to read about."

"I told them I wouldn't use their real names." Sadie sniffed. "I don't know what all the fuss is about."

"Look, everyone around here knows you've all been friends for years. If you put out a book that's semi-autobiographical, they're bound to wonder if the characters are based on real people. And who do you think they'll look to? You really should reconsider, Sadie. It'd be for the best, I'm sure."

Sadie shook her head. "Why should I? After the way they all turned on me, they deserve it—I shall never forgive them." She shook her hair from her shoulders. "You and Malcolm are the only ones who care about me." She looked around the room. "Where *is* Malcolm?"

"He was in the pub when I left. Don't worry about him, he'll come home when he's ready—he loves it there, what with everyone fussing over him. He'll be in no rush to get back." Ellie stood up and groaned as her knees creaked. "Right, I'm going to get something to eat—you want anything?"

"No, I've completely lost my appetite. I think I'll just have a shower and an early night."

"Okay, I'll leave you to it. I'll put some food down for Malcolm in case he comes back tonight and I'll leave your bedroom door ajar so he can get in. See you in the morning."

ooooooo

Sadie stood at her bedroom window, turning her face to the breeze that fluttered her kaftan.

She'd thought long and hard about the events of the evening. And her inability to forgive and forget had forced her hand.

I'll show them. I'm going to write this book so that no one who reads it is in any doubt about who the characters are based on. Call themselves friends? I'll teach them to gang up on me.

She closed her eyes but quickly opened them again to stop the room from spinning.

Why do I drink so much?

Clutching at the Georgian chest of drawers, the comfortable couches and the antique bureau at which she created her novels, she made her way to the dressing table and sat on the velvet upholstered stool.

She surveyed her reflection as she brushed her hair, so naturally glossy it gleamed even in the dim glow cast by the night light. Her cheeks were pink against her pale skin. Too pink, in her opinion. She always looked like she'd just run a marathon. And, of course, the drink didn't help.

As they often did, her thoughts drifted to the man she loved. Still loved, after all these years. She'd accepted that there was no chance of them ever being together now. And she'd kept tight-lipped about his identity.

A sudden movement startled her but she relaxed when she felt the silky coat of her Siamese cat rub against her ankles. "Oh, Malcolm. I'm so glad you've come back—I'm sorry I came home without you."

The cat gave her a haughty stare before padding off and slinking his sleek form through the narrow opening of the door.

Sadie sighed and promised herself for the umpteenth time that she'd get her act together. If she wasn't careful, she'd turn Malcolm against her, too—a scenario that simply didn't bear thinking about.

Her steps were heavy as she walked towards the turned down bed and lay on the cool sheet.

As she battled to keep her eyes from closing, it took only five minutes for her to lose the fight and succumb to her weariness, the breeze swaying the curtain back and forth as she drifted off to sleep.

If she'd only waited at the window for a minute longer, she might have seen the lone figure watching her from the shadow of the large elm tree at the end of the street...

Chapter 1

The four friends were gathered in the bedroom; three lounging on the bed around a box of chocolates, and one applying the finishing touches to her make up at the dressing table.

"Oh no! There's been another murder in St. Matlock."

Betty Tubbs read aloud from the local newspaper. "The body of a woman was discovered in the living room of her St. Matlock home early on Thursday morning. Although police have not identified the woman, nor have they released any further details, unconfirmed rumours suggest that she may be the latest victim of the St.

Matlock Murderer, who has already claimed the lives of four other women, and who remains at large.

"A previous victim who was lucky to escape with severe injuries, but who has since fully recovered, has given the only solid information regarding her attacker which is that he was wearing a long, dark coat with a hood and a fishnet stocking over his face during the assault. Thankfully, he was interrupted by the victim's daughter's early arrival home from work and he fled the scene through the back door.

"Despite the meticulous efforts of the forensics team, so far, they haven't found any DNA at any of the murder scenes which point to the identity of the perpetrator. All we know for sure is that, whoever the St. Matlock Murderer is, they've been ultra-careful to cover their tracks.

"The only clues the killer leaves behind are the silk ties he leaves wrapped around the necks of his victims and—"

"Oh, Betty, for goodness' sake! Can we change the subject, please? I've gone all goose bumpy." Harriett Lawley fanned her face with the lid of the chocolate box, her strawberry blonde waves lifting and falling in the draught. "I'd really rather not think about a murderer on the loose before a night out. Even if he *is* in the next town, it's still too close for comfort as far as I'm concerned."

"Well, *I've* got a story for you that'll take your mind off it." Ava Whittington ran a comb through her sleek, steel-grey bob. "There was quite a kerfuffle in The St. Eves' Tavern last night, so Alfonso told me when I was in the salon earlier. Sadie Grey was throwing punches, apparently."

"Honestly! What sort of behaviour is that for a fifty-seven year old woman? I know she likes to be noticed but, really, you'd think she'd know better." Harriett perused the chocolate box menu before selecting a fondant-dipped cherry and passing the box to Betty.

"Hmm, she's always liked to be the centre of attention, hasn't she? And quite volatile, from what I know of her. I don't think it takes a lot for her to lose her temper." Betty put down the newspaper, her eyes narrowing as she scoured the box for a hazelnut truffle. "And, according to Sheila in the bank, she's been a lot worse since she's become so successful. Takes great delight in telling everyone in a loud voice how much money's in her account. Thinks she's better than everyone else, apparently. What prompted the outburst, do you know?"

Ava held up a mirror behind her to check the back of her hair and shrugged a shoulder. "No idea but, according to Alfonso, she took exception to something that was said at her book launch celebration. He was in the pub having a quiet drink with his stylist and Sadie was there with a group of friends. He didn't hear what was said to upset her but, whatever it was, she went berserk—swearing and shouting at everyone, and then she punched Keith and vomited all over him." Ava screwed up her nose in distaste.

Charlotte Costello popped a salted almond caramel into her mouth. "Ew, how disgusting. Poor Keith. I bet Beverley was furious—you know how mad she gets if anyone has a go at him."

As Ava put her hand over her eyes and sprayed her hair liberally, Charlotte rolled across the bed to dodge the cloud of sticky mist heading her way. She picked up Sadie's latest book from Ava's bedside table, and read aloud from the fly leaf on which the author had penned a note.

"'To dear Ava, I do hope you'll enjoy my latest offering—if only walls had ears, they'd be blushing!'"

"She wrote that because some of it's a bit saucy. You know…it's got a little," Ava lowered her voice to a whisper, "s.e.x. in it."

"Oh, right. I see," said Charlotte, grinning at Ava's uncharacteristic coyness.

"Not all her books are like that, mind you, just this one—well, so far anyway. She usually writes crime novels but she's branching out to a new audience. She wanted to try her hand at something a little more…shall we say, racy. We queued at her book signing for over an hour, didn't we Harriett? We always like to support local talent, as you know. Anyway, she was absolutely charming, which is why it's so hard to imagine her making such a spectacle of herself in public."

"Hmm, I agree." Harriett nodded. "She was delightful. Very dramatic, too. You know what I mean? Loud and flamboyant, like a lot of creative people can be. And she looks at you so intently when she speaks to you—like her eyes are boring right through you. I wasn't sure if it made me feel special or unsettled."

"Creative types are like that," said Ava, with authority. "It's as though they have the gift of looking right into your soul."

"What *are* you talking about?" Harriett scoffed. "Honestly! You talk such poppycock sometimes, Ava."

"Well, I've *never* liked her." Betty's usually placid demeanour was unusually ruffled. "She's always been a bit above herself, if you ask me. I told you that she completely ignored me in the organic food shop recently, didn't I? I was in the middle of speaking to her and she just talked over me and ordered four lemon muffins and a malt loaf. I felt like such an idiot. I can assure you, I won't bother chatting with her again. I've got no time for people who get ideas above their station."

The most gentle and courteous of the three women, Charlotte had never known Betty to disrespect anyone and she felt a wave of affection for her old friend.

"Anyway, wasn't she asked to leave the St. Eves' Ladies' Association a few years ago?" Betty helped herself to another hazelnut truffle and resumed her browsing of the newspaper. "Because of her drinking?"

Harriett nodded. "They got fed up with her turning up to meetings completely inebriated so they took a vote to get rid of her. It was almost unanimous, apparently. Everyone but three of her friends voted to have her kicked out and the committee went with the majority. It must have been terribly difficult for them, being put in a position like that."

"Ooh, listen to this!" Betty licked the chocolate from her teeth and held the newspaper at arm's length. "'Local author, Sadie Grey, thrilled crowds at her recent book signing event when she hinted that, following the huge success of her first risqué novel, a second titillating offering may be in the pipeline.

"'However, our source has revealed that the second book may not be a complete work of fiction; rathermore a collection of memoirs intertwined with semi-fictional characters which will reveal the antics and aspirations of Sadie as a younger woman. This news is certain to put the proverbial cat amongst the pigeons as Sadie has promised that the book will be a no-holds-barred account of her life, which, if the rumours are true, will spill the beans on the exploits of certain members of the St. Eves' community, a number of whom have been close friends of Sadie's for decades.'"

"Well that explains it," said Harriett. "If her new book's going to lift the lid on what she and her friends got up to years ago, goodness only knows what secrets she may be about to divulge that they'd rather she kept to herself. I wouldn't be at all surprised if that was the reason for the bust-up."

"Hmm, could be." Ava studied her reflection from every angle in the three-way dressing table mirror. "By the way, Harriett, any news on when you and Leo are getting the keys for your new place yet?"

Harriett's cheeks flushed. "Yes, next week. I'm so excited, I can hardly wait."

There'd been much debate in recent months about whether Harriett and her companion, Leo Reeves, should decide to take the plunge and start looking for a retirement bungalow to move into, but the decision had been made for them when the place next to Betty had become available following the death of its nonagenarian resident.

As soon as Harriett had heard the news, she'd spoken to Leo and they'd decided to put down a holding deposit on the bungalow and put their own houses up for sale.

"Fate's on our side, love!" Leo had said when, in the space of two weeks, their properties were snapped up by buyers, eager to put down roots in St. Eves. "It's obviously meant to be."

Until the sale went through, they were living with their good friend, Harry Jenkins, who'd offered to put them up until the purchase of the bungalow had been completed.

Charlotte leaned across the bed and gave Harriett's hand a squeeze. "That's fantastic! You're going to be so happy there, I just know it."

"And what are you doing about getting the place decorated? Is Leo going to do it or are you hiring someone?" Ava re-applied a slick of *Caribbean Sunset* and smacked her lips together.

"We're definitely hiring someone." Harriett's tone was firm. "Leo only has to look at a paintbrush and a ladder to bring on a bilious attack. He can turn his hand to many things but decorating certainly isn't one of them. We're going to start looking through the Yellow Pages and classified ads tomorrow."

"I expect it'll be nice to have a place of your own again, after staying with Harry for so long?" said Betty.

Harriett nodded. "Harry's been wonderful, but I can't pretend it hasn't been a strain, all of us living together in the same house. I mean, it's only got two bedrooms and he's given them to Leo and I while he sleeps on the sofa bed. Leo insisted that he'd take it but Harry wouldn't hear of it. He said, 'What kind of friend lets their best pal sleep on a sofa bed?'

"It's awfully kind of him to have been so hospitable but it can't have been easy for him when he's become as accustomed to having his own space as Leo and I have to ours. We're so grateful to him for putting us up but we can't wait to get into our own place.

"We weren't anticipating getting somewhere together quite so soon—I didn't think our own places would sell for ages—but everything's moved so fast. Anyway, as soon as the place has been decorated and furnished, we'll move in."

"Have you decided on the sleeping arrangements?" Ava blotted her lipstick on a tissue and squirted herself with an abundance of Lily of the Valley.

"*Ava!*" Harriett's face turned crimson and she fanned herself again with the chocolate box lid. "For heaven's sake! It's none of your business! Honestly, one of these days, someone's going to cut the end of that nose off if you're not careful."

"What have I said?" Ava's eyes widened as she held out her hands, palms upward. "So many couples are choosing to sleep apart these days, it's a perfectly reasonable curiosity to be contemplating. And I don't know why you're so shy in front of us—we've been friends since we were tots."

"She's right, you know." Betty took another bitter orange whirl from the tray. "I know if I met a man I wanted to spend the rest of my days with, I can assure you, I wouldn't waste any time getting to know him under the covers…heehee." She wheezed and chuckled simultaneously.

"*Stop!*" An unusually flustered Harriett held out her hands and stood up. "Not that it's *any* of your business but we'll be sleeping in separate rooms. And that's the end of the discussion." She looked at her watch. "Surely it must be time to leave?" She muttered under her breath, "Please, God."

Ava and Betty cast a sideways glance at each other and grinned.

"Right. Enough chat, we must be off. Are you ready, dear?"

Charlotte picked up her car keys. "Ready when you are."

Half an hour later, she pulled up outside the theatre that was hosting the dance competition in which Ava's husband was competing.

"Didn't you say Derek's got a new dance partner? She's quite young, isn't she? Is he dancing with her today?"

Ava nodded. "Well, she's young by my standards. She's forty-two. Her usual partner went off to Cuba to study Latin-American dance and, apart from running a few salsa classes, she's been at a loose end since then. Still, it meant she was free to step in and take over where Rita left off. I only hope to God she'll be as good as Rita—trust her to go and get hit by a motorbike six weeks before the competition. She's going to be alright, thank goodness, but I do hope Derek isn't too nervous without her." Ava unfastened her seat belt. "His right heel taps uncontrollably when he is. I tell you, my dears, it'll play havoc with his Viennese Waltz."

Betty chuckled. "D'you remember when we went to see him in that competition and he'd only had two days to learn the steps to his routine because he'd been in bed with man flu? Remember, Ava? His heel was tapping so much, we thought he was about to launch into a rendition of Riverdance."

Harriett giggled but stopped abruptly as Ava cut her short with a glare in the vanity mirror. She was terribly sensitive about husband Derek and his dancing.

"Yes, I don't need reminding, thank you, Betty." Ava sniffed through flared nostrils. "Right, come on, let's get inside or he'll think we're not coming and go into tapping overdrive. Thank you for the lift, Charlotte, dear, it's very kind of you. And give Molly a big hug from me."

"I will. And I'll keep my fingers crossed for Derek. Hope he wins."

OTHER BOOKS BY SHERRI BRYAN

The Charlotte Denver Cozy Mystery Series
Tapas, Carrot Cake and a Corpse - 1
Fudge Cake, Felony and a Funeral - 2
Spare Ribs, Secrets and a Scandal - 3
Pumpkins, Peril and a Paella - 4
Hamburgers, Homicide and a Honeymoon - 5
Crab Cakes, Killers and a Kaftan - 6
Mince Pies, Mistletoe and Murder - 7
Doughnuts, Diamonds and Dead Men - 8
Bread, Dead and Wed – 9

The Bliss Bay Village Mystery Series
Bodies, Baddies and a Crabby Tabby - 1
Secrets, Lies and Puppy Dog Eyes - 2
Malice, Remorse and a Rocking Horse - 3
Dormice, Schemers and Misdemeanours - 4

Sherri Bryan

A Selection of Recipes from this Book

Grandma Doris's Boiled Fruit Cake

Ingredients
2 medium eggs, beaten
1 cup sugar
8 oz butter or margarine
1½ cups dried, mixed fruit of your choice, plus ½ cup dried (or glacé) cherries or cranberries
1 cup water
1 teaspoon bicarbonate of soda
½ teaspoon mixed spice
1 cup plain flour
1½ cups self-raising flour

Method
1. Place fruit (except the cherries or cranberries), sugar, butter and water into a saucepan of cold water, bring to a boil and cook for five minutes.
2. After five minutes, transfer the mixture to a mixing bowl to cool.
3. When cool, add the bicarbonate of soda, mixed spice and beaten eggs to the mixture and mix everything together.
4. Fold in the flour, a spoonful at a time, before adding the cherries or cranberries.
5. Line and lightly grease a seven inch baking tin and pour in the mixture.

6. Bake in the middle of a preheated oven at 325°F/170°C/Gas 3, for 1 - 1¼ hours, or until a

skewer inserted into the middle of the cake comes out clean.

7. Allow to cool before slicing.

Charlotte's Chicken Casserole with Dumplings
Serves four to six people

Ingredients
1 whole chicken, jointed into eight pieces
6 rashers of smoked bacon, chopped
25g/1oz butter
225g/8oz whole baby onions, peeled
1 teaspoon mixed herbs or a bouquet garni of thyme, bay leaves, peppercorns, rosemary sprigs and a celery stalk
800ml/27 fl oz chicken stock
2 tablespoons vegetable oil
2 medium onions, peeled and chopped
2 leeks, washed and sliced
3 large carrots, chopped
2 potatoes, peeled and chopped
2 bay leaves (use these even if you are using a bouquet garni)
Salt and pepper to season
Chopped parsley to garnish

For the dumplings
250g/8 ½ oz self-raising flour
125g/4 ¼ oz cold butter, straight from the fridge
100ml/3 fl oz cold water

Method
1. Preheat your oven to 170°C/325°F/Gas mark 3
2. Heat the oil in a large cast-iron casserole dish, or frying pan, and fry the chicken pieces, in batches, until brown. Transfer them to a plate.

3. Gently fry the bacon pieces in the same pan and then put them on the plate with the chicken.
4. Add the butter to the oil in the casserole and gently cook the onions until they become soft and golden brown.
5. Add the chicken and bacon back to the casserole.
6. Add the carrots, leeks, potatoes, bay leaves, herbs or bouquet garni and chicken stock to the dish and season well.
7. Cover with a lid and put into the centre of the preheated oven to cook for 40 minutes.
8. While the casserole is cooking, make the dumplings as follows:
9. Put the self-raising flour into a mixing bowl with a pinch of salt.
10. Coarsely grate the cold butter and rub it together with the flour until it resembles breadcrumbs.
11. Add the cold water to the flour and butter and mix together gently until you form a ball of dough. (Note: Don't knead the dough too vigorously—it only needs a gentle bringing together with your hands until it's all combined).
12. Divide the dough into twelve and roll into balls.
13. At the end of the 40 minutes cooking time, carefully take the casserole from the oven and place the dumplings on top.
14. Replace the lid and return the casserole to the oven for a further 30 minutes, after which, the

dumplings should be cooked through and fluffy and the chicken, meltingly tender.
15. Sprinkle with freshly chopped parsley and serve.

Hamburgers, Homicide and a Honeymoon

Big Al's Burgers
Serves four very hungry people

Ingredients
800g/1lb chuck steak mince, coarsely ground (I've found that between 25% and 30% fat content in the meat makes the tastiest, juiciest burgers—even if you like them very well done—and it helps them stay together). **Note:** If you can, ask your butcher to mince the chuck steak for you. If you can't, you can buy ready minced meat
1 large onion, finely chopped
4 anchovy fillets from a can or a jar (secret ingredient) + 1 tablespoon vegetable oil
110g/4oz mature cheddar cheese, grated
Salt and freshly ground black pepper
2 tablespoons vegetable oil for frying
4 burger buns
Mayonnaise, ketchup and/or mustard and sliced tomatoes, lettuce and pickles to serve, if required

Method
1. Divide the cheese into four and form into balls. Put into the fridge until needed.
2. Put the anchovy fillets into a small bowl with the tablespoon of vegetable oil. Mash them with a spoon until they break up and 'dissolve' into the oil.
3. Place the minced meat into a large bowl.
4. Drizzle the anchovy/oil mix evenly over the meat and add the chopped onion and salt and pepper. (**Note:** you won't need as much salt as

Page 233

you may normally add because the anchovies are quite salty).

5. Mix everything together with your hands—it's a little messy but it's the best way to combine all the ingredients.

6. Divide the mince mixture into four and form into flat patties, making sure to leave a well in the middle.

7. Put a cheese ball into each well and mould the meat around it until all the cheese is covered.

8. Flatten the burgers a little with your hands or with a fish slice.

9. Heat the remaining vegetable oil in a non-stick frying pan over a medium heat and brown the burgers on both sides.

10. Keeping an eye on them, cook the burgers gently for between twenty-five and thirty minutes, flipping a couple of times during cooking. (**Note:** If you have a pan with a heatproof handle, you can cook the burgers in the oven which has been preheated to 180°C/350°F/Gas 4, if you prefer, but don't forget to use an oven glove to take the pan out!)

11. When the burgers are cooked to your liking, slice the buns and spread each half with mayonnaise, ketchup or mustard. Add the burger and fill the buns with additional ingredients if required before serving.

Note from Sherri

Hello, and thanks for reading Hamburgers, Homicide and a Honeymoon, the fifth book in The Charlotte Denver Cozy Mystery Series.

If you've read the other books in the series, you'll notice that this book is a little different in that it's the first time I've taken the protagonists out of their comfort zone. And mine, too!

Whilst I have tried to be accurate throughout, for dramatic purposes, my imagination may have called for actual facts and procedures to be slightly 'skewed' from time to time, and I hope this didn't detract from your enjoyment of the story.

As with all my books, this one has been proofread and edited many times but—as is sometimes the case when humans are involved—there may be still be the odd mistake within its pages. If you should come across one, my apologies, and I'd be grateful if you could let me know so I can put it right.

You can contact me by email at sherri@sherribryan.com, or on Facebook at https://www.facebook.com/sherribryanauthor.

Thanks again for taking an interest in my book—I appreciate it very much.

I hope you'll enjoy the rest of the series.
Sending best wishes,
Sherri Bryan.

Sherri Bryan

About Sherri Bryan

Sherri lives in Spain.

Apart from writing, her main interests include cooking, reading and spending time with friends and family.

When she's not tapping away on her keyboard, you'll most likely find her cooking up something experimental in the kitchen, curled up with her nose in a book, or dreaming up new cozy mystery plots.

ACKNOWLEDGEMENTS

A huge virtual hug, and a heartfelt thank you, to everyone who has followed Charlotte and the rest of the St Eves' residents from book one, and to new readers who have only just discovered them.

And to Kimberly, my editor.

Sherri Bryan

ALL RIGHTS RESERVED

No part of this publication may be reproduced, distributed, or transmitted in any form, or by any means, including photocopying, recording, or other electronic or mechanical methods, without the prior written permission of the copyright owner, and publisher, of this piece of work, except in the case of brief quotations embodied in critical reviews.

This is a work of fiction. All names, characters, businesses, organizations, places, events and incidents are either the products of the author's imagination, or are used in an entirely fictitious manner.

Any other resemblance to organizations, actual events or actual persons, living or dead, is purely coincidental.

Published by Sherri Bryan - Copyright ©2016